D1051834

BOOKS BY **A. S. BYATT**

A. S. BYATT'S

The Matisse Stories

A. S. Byatt is the author of *Possession*, winner of the
Booker Prize and a national bestseller. She has taught
English and American literature at University
College, London, and is a distinguished critic and
reviewer. Her other fiction includes *The Shadow of
the Sun*, *The Game*, *The Virgin in the Garden*, *Still
Life*, *Sugar and Other Stories*, *Angels & Insects*, and
Babel Tower. She has also published three volumes of
critical work, of which *Passions of the Mind* is the
most recent. She lives in London.

INTERNATIONAL

The Matisse Stories

A. S. BYATT

VINTAGE INTERNATIONAL

Vintage Books

A Division of Random House, Inc.

New York

FIRST VINTAGE INTERNATIONAL EDITION, APRIL 1996

The Library of Congress has cataloged
the Random House edition as follows:
Byatt, A. S. (Antonia Susan)
The Matisse stories / A. S. Byatt
p. cm.
ISBN 0-679-43882-3
1. Matisse, Henri, 1869-1954. I. Title.
PR6052.Y2M37 1993
823'.914—dc20 94-46131
Vintage ISBN: 0-679-76223-x

Random House Web address: http://www.randomhouse.com/

Printed in the United States of America
10 9 8 7 6 5 4 3 2 1

For Peter

Who taught me to look at things slowly.

With love.

Contents

Medusa's Ankles

La chevelure, 1931-32

Medusa's Ankles

She had walked in one day because she had seen the Rosy Nude through the plate glass. That was odd, she thought, to have that lavish and complex creature stretched voluptuously above the coat rack, where one might have expected the stare, silver and supercilious or jetty and frenzied, of the model girl. They were all girls now, not women. The rosy nude was pure flat colour, but suggested mass. She had huge haunches and a monumental knee, lazily propped high. She had round breasts, contemplations of the circle, reflections on flesh and its fall.

She had asked cautiously for a cut and blow-dry. He had done her himself, the owner, Lucian of 'Lucian's', slender and soft-moving, resembling a balletic Hamlet with full white sleeves and tight black trousers. The first few times she came it was the trousers she remembered, better than his face, which she saw only in the mirror behind her own, and which she felt a middle-aged disinclination to study. A woman's relation with her hairdresser is anatomically odd. Her face meets his belt, his haunches skim her breathing, his face is far away, high and behind. His face had a closed and monkish look, rather fine, she thought, under soft, straight, dark hair, bright with health, not with added fats, or so it seemed.

'I like your Matisse,' she said, the first time.

He looked blank.

'The pink nude. I love her.'

'Oh, that. I saw it in a shop. I thought it went exactly with the colour-scheme I was planning.'

Their eyes met in the mirror.

'I thought she was wonderful,' he said. 'So calm, so damn sure of herself, such a lovely colour, I do think, don't you? I fell for her, absolutely. I saw her in this shop in the Charing Cross Road and I went home, and said to my wife, I might think of placing her in the salon, and she thought nothing to it, but the next day I went back and just got her. She gives the salon a bit of class. I like things to have class.'

In those days the salon was like the interior of a rosy cloud, all pinks and creams, with creamy muslin curtains here and there, and ivory brushes and combs, and here and there—the mirror-frames, the little trollies—a kind of sky blue, a dark sky blue, the colour of the couch or bed on which the rosy nude spread herself. Music played—Susannah hated piped music—but this music was tinkling and tripping and dropping, quiet seraglio music, like sherbet. He gave her coffee in pink cups, with a pink and white wafer biscuit in the saucer. He soothed her middle-aged hair into a cunningly blown and natural windswept sweep, with escaping strands and tendrils, softening brow and chin. She remembered the hairdressing shop of her wartime childhood, with its boarded wooden cubicles, its advertisements for Amami shampoo, depicting ladies with blonde pageboys and red lips, in the forties bow which was wider than the thirties rosebud. Amami, she had always supposed, rhymed with smarmy and was somehow related to it. When she became a linguist, and could decline the verb to love in several languages, she saw suddenly one day that Amami was an erotic invitation, or command. Amami, love me, the blondes said, under their impeccably massed rolls of hair. Her mother had gone draggled under the chipped dome of the hairdryer, bristling with metal rollers, bobby-pins and pipe-cleaners. And had come out under a rigidly bouncy 'set', like a mountain of wax fruit, that made her seem artificial and embarrassing, drawing attention somehow to the unnatural whiteness of her false teeth.

They had seemed like some kind of electrically shocking initiation into womanhood, those clamped domes descending and engulfing. She remembered her own first 'set', the heat and buzzing, and afterwards a slight torn tenderness of the scalp, a slight tindery dryness to the hair.

In the sixties and seventies she had kept a natural look, had grown her hair long and straight and heavy, a chestnut-glossy curtain, had avoided places like this. And in the years of her avoidance, the cubicles had gone, everything was open and shared and above board, blow-dryers had largely replaced the hoods, plastic spikes the bristles.

She had had to come back because her hair began to grow old. The ends split, the weight of it broke, a kind of frizzed fur replaced the gloss. Lucian said that curls and waves—following the lines of the new unevenness—would dissimulate, would render natural-looking, that was, young, what was indeed natural, the death of the cells. Short and bouncy was best, Lucian said, and proved it, tactfully. He stood above her with his fine hands cupped lightly round her new bubbles and wisps, like the hands of a priest round a Grail. She looked, quickly, quickly, it was better than before, thanked him and averted her eyes.

She came to trust him with her disintegration.

He was always late to their appointment, to all appointments. The salon was full of whisking young things, male and female, and he stopped to speak to all of them, to all the patient sitters, with their questing, mirror-bound stares. The telephone rang perpetually. She sat on a rosy foamy pouffe and read in a glossy magazine, *Her Hair*, an article at once solemnly portentous and remorselessly jokey (such tones are common) about the hairdresser as the new healer, with his cure of souls.

Once, the magazine informed her, the barber had been the local surgeon, had drawn teeth, set bones and dealt with female problems. Now in the rush of modern alienated life, the hairdresser performed the all-important function of listening. He elicited the tale of your troubles and calmed you.

Lucian did not. He had another way. He created his own psychiatrist and guru from his captive hearer. Or at least, so Susannah found, who may have been specially selected because she was plump, which could be read as motherly, and because, as a university teacher she was, as he detected, herself a professional listener. He asked her advice.

'I don't see myself shut in here for the next twenty years. I want more out of life. Life has to have a meaning. I tried Tantric Art and the School of Meditation. Do you know about that sort of thing, about the inner life?'

His fingers flicked and flicked in her hair, he compressed a ridge and scythed it.

'Not really. I'm an agnostic.'

'I'd like to know about art. You know about art. You know about that pink nude, don't you? How do I find out?'

She told him to read Lawrence Gowing, and he clamped the tress he was attending to, put down his scissors, and wrote it all down in a little dove-grey leather book. She told him where to find good extra-mural classes and who was good among the gallery lecturers.

Next time she came it was not art, it was archaeology. There was no evidence that he had gone to the galleries or read the books.

'The past pulls you,' he said. 'Bones in the ground and gold coins in a hoard, all that. I went down to the City and saw them digging up the Mithraic temples. There's a religion, all that bull's blood, dark and light, fascinating.'

She wished he would tidy her head and be quiet. She could recognise the flitting mind, she considered. It frightened her. What she knew, what she cared about, what was coherent, was separate shards for him to flit over, remaining separate. You wrote books and gave lectures, and these little ribbons of fact shone briefly and vanished.

'I don't want to put the best years of my life into making suburban old dears presentable,' he said. 'I want something more.'

'What?' she said, meeting his brooding stare above the wet mat of her mop. He puffed foam into it and said, 'Beauty, I want beauty. I must have beauty. I want to sail on a yacht among the Greek isles, with beautiful people.' He caught her eye. 'And see those temples and those sculptures.' He pressed close, he pushed at the nape of her neck, her nose was near his discreet zip.

'You've been washing it without conditioner,' he said. 'You aren't doing yourself any good. I can tell.'

She bent her head submissively, and he scraped the base of her skull.

'You could have highlights,' he said in a tone of no enthusiasm. 'Bronze or mixed autumnal.'

'No thanks. I prefer it natural.'

He sighed.

He began to tell her about his love life. She would have inclined, on the evidence before her eyes, to the view that he was homosexual. The salon was full of beautiful young men, who came, wielded the scissors briefly, giggled together in corners, and departed. Chinese, Indonesian, Glaswegian, South African. He shouted at them and giggled with them, they exchanged little gifts and paid off obscure little debts to each other. Once she came in late and found them sitting in a circle, playing poker. The girls were subordinate and brightly hopeless. None of them lasted long. They wore—in those days— pink overalls with cream silk bindings. She could tell he had a love life because of the amount of time he spent alternately pleasing and blustering on the telephone, his voice a blotting-paper hiss, his words inaudible, though she could hear the peppery rattle of the other voice, or voices, in the ear-piece. Her sessions began to take a long time, what with these phone calls and with his lengthy explanations, which he would accompany with gestures, making her look at his mirrored excitement, like a boy riding a bicycle with hands off.

'Forgive me if I'm a bit distracted,' he said. 'My life is in crisis. Something I never believed could happen has happened. All my life I've been looking for something and now I've found it.'

He wiped suds casually from her wet brow and scraped her eye-corner. She blinked.

'Love,' he said. 'Total affinity. Absolute compatibility. A miracle. My other half. A perfectly beautiful girl.'

She could think of no sentence to answer this. She

said, schoolmistressy, what other tone was there? 'And this has caused the crisis?'

'She loves me, I couldn't believe it but it is true. She loves me. She wants me to live with her.'

'And your wife?'

There was a wife, who had thought nothing to the purchase of the Rosy Nude.

'She told me to get out of the house. So I got out. I went to her flat—my girlfriend's. She came and fetched me back—my wife. She said I must choose, but she thinks I'll choose her. I said it would be better for the moment just to let it evolve. I told her how do I know what I want, in this state of ecstasy, how do I know it'll last, how do I know she'll go on loving me?'

He frowned impatiently and waved the scissors dangerously near her temples.

'All she cares about is respectability. She says she loves me but all she cares about is what the neighbours say. I like my house, though. She keeps it nice, I have to say. It's not stylish, but it is in good taste.'

Over the next few months, maybe a year, the story evolved, in bumps and jerks, not, it must be said, with any satisfactory narrative shape. He was a very bad storyteller, Susannah realised slowly. None of the characters acquired any roundness. She formed no image of the nature of the beauty of the girlfriend, or of the way she spent her time when not demonstrating her total affinity for Lucian. She did not know whether the wife was a shrew or a sufferer, nervous or patient or even ironically detached. All these wraith-personae were inventions of Susannah's own. About six months through the narrative Lucian said that his daughter was very upset about it all, the way he was forced to come and go, sometimes living at home, sometimes shut out.

'You have a daughter?'

'Fifteen. No, seventeen, I always get ages wrong!'

She watched him touch his own gleaming hair in the mirror, and smile apprehensively at himself.

'We were married very young,' he said. 'Very young, before we knew what was what.'

'It's hard on young girls, when there are disputes at home.'

'It is. It's hard on everyone. She says if I sell the house she'll have nowhere to live while she takes her exams. I have to sell the house if I'm to afford to keep up my half of my girlfriend's flat. I can't keep up the mortgages on both. My wife doesn't want to move. It's understandable, I suppose, but she has to see we can't go on like this. I can't be torn apart like this, I've got to decide.'

'You seem to have decided for your girlfriend.'

He took a deep breath and put down everything, comb, scissors, hairdryer.

'Ah, but I'm scared. I'm scared stiff if I take the plunge, I'll be left with nothing. If she's got me all the time, my girlfriend, perhaps she won't go on loving me like this. And I like my house, you know, it feels sort of comfortable to me, I'm used to it, all the old chairs. I don't quite like to think of it all sold and gone.'

'Love isn't easy.'

'You can say that again.'

'Do you think I'm getting thinner on top?'

'What? Oh no, not really, I wouldn't worry. We'll just train this little bit to fall across there like that. Do you think she has a right to more than half the value of the house?'

'I'm not a lawyer. I'm a classicist.'

'We're going on that Greek holiday. Me and my girlfriend. Sailing through the Greek Isles. I've bought scuba gear. The salon will be closed for a month.'

'I'm glad you told me.'

While he was away the salon was redecorated. He had not told her about this, also, as indeed, why should he have done? It was done very fashionably in the latest colours, battleship-grey and maroon. Dried blood and instruments of slaughter, Susannah thought on her return. The colour scheme was one she particularly disliked. Everything was changed. The blue trollies had been replaced with hi-tech steely ones, the ceiling lowered, the faintly aquarial plate glass was replaced with storm-grey-one-way-see-through-no-glare which made even bright days dull ones. The music was now muted heavy metal. The young men and young women wore dark grey Japanese wrappers and what she thought of as the patients, which included herself, wore identical maroon ones. Her face in the mirror was grey, had lost the deceptive rosy haze of the earlier lighting.

The Rosy Nude was taken down. In her place were photographs of girls with grey faces, coal-black eyes and spiky lashes, under bonfires of incandescent puce hair which matched their lips, rounded to suck, at microphones perhaps, or other things. The new teacups were black and hexagonal. The pink flowery biscuits were replaced by sugar-coated minty elliptical sweets, black and white like Go counters. She thought after the first shock of this, that she would go elsewhere. But she was afraid of being made, accidentally, by anyone else, to look a fool. He understood her hair, Lucian, she told herself. It needed understanding, these days, it was not much any more, its life was fading from it.

'Did you have a good holiday?'

'Oh idyllic. Oh yes, a dream. I wish I hadn't come back. She's been to a solicitor. Claiming the matrimonial home for all the work she's done on it, and because of my daughter. I say, what about when she grows up, she'll get a job, won't she? You can't assume she'll hang around mummy for ever, they don't.'

'I need to look particularly good this time. I've won a prize. A Translator's Medal. I have to make a speech. On television.'

'We'll have to make you look lovely, won't we? For

the honour of the salon. How do you like our new look?'

'It's very smart.'

'It is. It is. I'm not quite satisfied with the photos, though. I thought we could get something more intriguing. It has to be photos to go with the grey.'

He worked above her head. He lifted her wet hair with his fingers and let the air run through it, as though there was twice as much as there was. He pulled a twist this way, and clamped it to her head, and screwed another that way, and put his head on one side and another, contemplating her uninspiring bust. When her head involuntarily followed his he said quite nastily, 'Keep still, can you, I can't work if you keep bending from side to side like a swan.'

'I'm sorry.'

'No harm done, just keep still.'

She kept still as a mouse, her head bowed under his repressing palm. She turned up her eyes and saw him look at his watch, then, with a kind of balletic movement of wrists, scissors and finger-points above her brow, drive the sharp steel into the ball of his thumb, so that blood spurted, so that some of his blood even fell on to her scalp.

'Oh dear. Will you excuse me? I've cut myself. Look.'

He waved the bloody member before her nose.

'I saw,' she said. 'I saw you cut yourself.'

He smiled at her in the mirror, a glittery smile, not meeting her eyes.

'It's a little trick we hairdressers have. When we've been driving ourselves and haven't had time for a bite or a breather, we get cut, and off we go, to the toilet, to take a bite of Mars Bar or a cheese roll if the receptionist's been considerate. Will you excuse me? I am faint for lack of food.'

'Of course,' she said.

He flashed his glass smile at her and slid away.

She waited. A little water dripped into her collar. A little more ran into her eyebrows. She looked at her poor face, under its dank cap and its two random corkscrews, aluminium clamped. She felt a gentle protective rage towards this stolid face. She remembered, not as a girl, as a young woman under all that chestnut fall, looking at her skin, and wondering how it could grow into the crêpe, the sag, the opulent soft bags. This was her face, she had thought then. And this, too, now, she wanted to accept for her face, trained in a respect for precision, and could not. What had left this greying skin, these flakes, these fragile stretches with no elasticity, was her, was her life, was herself. She had never been a beautiful woman, but she had been attractive, with the attraction of liveliness and warm energy, of the flow of quick blood and brightness of eye. No classic bones, which might endure, no fragile bird-like sharpness that might whitely go forward. Only the life of flesh, which began to die.

She was in a panic of fear about the television, which had come too late, when she had lost the desire to be seen or looked at. The cameras search jowl and eye-pocket, expose brush-stroke and cracks in shadow and gloss. So interesting are their revelations that words, mere words, go for nothing, fly by whilst the memory of a chipped tooth, a strayed red dot, an inappropriate hair, persists and persists.

If he had not left her so long to contemplate her wet face, it might not have happened.

On either side of her mysteries were being enacted. On the left, a head was crammed into a pink nylon bag, something between a bank-robber's stocking and a monstrous Dutch cap. A young Chinese man was peacefully teasing threads of hair through the meshes of this with a tug and a flick, a tug and a flick. The effect was one of startling hideous pink baldness, tufted here and there. On her right, an anxious plump girl was rolling another girl's thick locks into snaky sausages of aluminium foil. There was a thrum of distant drums through the loudspeakers, a clash and crash of what sounded like shaken chains. It is all nonsense, she thought, I should go home, I can't, I am wet. They stared transfixed at their respective ugliness.

He came back, and took up the scissors, listlessly enough.

'How much did you want off?' he said casually. 'You've got a lot of broken ends. It's deteriorating, you haven't fed it while I've been away.'

'Not too much off, I want to look natural, I . . .'

'I've been talking to my girlfriend. I've decided. I shan't go back any more to my wife. I can't bear it.'

'She's too angry?'

'She's let herself go. It's her own fault. She's let herself go altogether. She's let her ankles get fat, they swell over her shoes, it disgusts me, it's impossible for me.'

'That happens to people. Fluid absorption . . .'

She did not look down at her own ankles. He had her by the short hairs at the nape of her neck.

'Lucian,' said the plump girl, plaintively, 'can you just take a look here at this perm, I can't seem to get the hang of this.'

'You'd better be careful,' said Lucian, 'or Madam'll go green and fry and you'll be in deep trouble. Why don't you just come and finish off Madam here—you don't mind, do you, dear? Deirdre is very good with your sort of hair, very tactful, I'm training her myself—I'd better take a look at this perm. It's a new method we're just trying out, we've had a few problems, you see how it is . . .'

Deirdre was an elicitor, but Susannah would not speak. Vaguely, far away, she heard the anxious little voice. 'Do you have children, dear, have you far to go home, how formal do you like it, do you want back-combing . . . ?' Susannah stared stony, thinking about Lucian's wife's ankles. Because her own ankles rubbed her shoes, her sympathies had to be with this unknown and ill-presented woman. She remembered with sudden total clarity a day when, Suzie then, not Susannah, she had made love all day to an Italian student on a course in Perugia. She remembered her own little round rosy breasts, her own long legs stretched over the side of the single bed, the hot, the wet, his shoulders, the clash of skulls as they tried to mix themselves completely. They had reached a point when neither of them could move, they had loved each other so much, they had tried to get up to get water, for they were dying of thirst, they were soaked with sweat and dry-mouthed, and they collapsed back upon the bed, naked skin on naked skin, unable to rise. What was this to anyone now? Rage rose in her, for the fat-ankled woman, like a red flood, up from her thighs across her chest, up her neck, it must flare like a flag in her face, but how to tell in this daft cruel grey light? Deirdre was rolling up curls, piling them up, who would have thought the old woman had so much hair on her head? Sausages and snail-shells, grape-clusters and twining coils. She could only see dimly, for the red flood was like a curtain at the back of her eyes, but she knew what she saw. The Japanese say demons of another world approach us through mirrors as fish rise through water, and, bubble-eyed and trailing fins, a fat demon swam towards her, turret-crowned, snake-crowned, her mother fresh from the dryer in all her embarrassing ir-reality.

'There,' said Deirdre. 'That's nice. I'll just get a mir-ror.'

'It isn't nice,' said Susannah. 'It's hideous.'

There was a hush in the salon. Deirdre turned a terri-fied gaze on Lucian.

'She did it better than I do, dear,' he said. 'She gave it a bit of lift. That's what they all want, these days. I think you look really nice.'

'It's horrible,' said Susannah. *'I look like a middle-aged woman with a hair-do.'*

She could see them all looking at each other, sharing the knowledge that this was exactly what she was.

'Not natural,' she said.

'I'll get Deirdre to tone it down,' said Lucian.

Susannah picked up a bottle, full of gel. She brought it down, heavily, on the grey glass shelf, which cracked.

'I don't want it toned down, I want,' she began, and stared mesmerised at the crack, which was smeared with gel.

'I want my real hair back,' Susannah cried, and thumped harder, shattering both shelf and bottle.

'Now, dear, I'm sorry,' said Lucian in a tone of sweet reason. She could see several of him, advancing on her; he was standing in a corner and was reflected from wall to wall, a cohort of slender, trousered swordsmen, waving the bright scissors like weapons.

'Keep away,' she said. 'Get off. Keep back.'

'Calm yourself,' said Lucian.

Susannah seized a small cylindrical pot and threw it at one of his emanations. It burst with a satisfying crash and one whole mirror became a spider-web of cracks, from which fell, tinkling, a little heap of crystal nuggets. In front of Susannah was a whole row of such bombs or grenades. She lobbed them all around her. Some of the cracks made a kind of strained singing noise, some were explosive. She whirled a container of hairpins about her head and scattered it like a nailbomb. She tore dryers from their sockets and sprayed the puce punk with sweet-smelling foam. She broke basins with brushes and tripped the young Chinese male, who was the only one not apparently petrified, with a hissing trolley, swaying dangerously and scattering puffs of cotton-wool and rattling trails of clips and tags. She silenced the blatter of the music with a well-aimed imitation alabaster pot of Juvenescence Emulsion, which dripped into the cassette which whirred more and more slowly in a thickening morass of blush-coloured cream.

When she had finished—and she went on, she kept going, until there was nothing else to hurl, for she was already afraid of what must happen when she had finished—there was complete human silence in the salon. There were strange, harshly musical sounds all round. A bowl rocking on a glass shelf. A pair of scissors, dancing on a hook, their frenzy diminishing. Uneven spasmodic falls of glass, like musical hailstones on shelves and floors. A susurration of hairpins on paper. A slow creaking of damaged panes. Her own hands were bleeding. Lucian advanced crunching over the shining silt, and dabbed at them with a towel. He too was bloodied—specks on his shirt, a fine dash on his brow, nothing substantial. It was a strange empty battlefield, full of glittering fragments and sweet-smelling rivulets and puddles of venous-blue and fuchsia-red unguents, patches of crimson-streaked foam and odd intense spills of orange henna or cobalt and copper.

'I'd better go,' she said, turning blindly with her bleeding hands, still in her uncouth maroon drapery.

'Deirdre'll make you a cup of coffee,' said Lucian. 'You'd better sit down and take a breather.'

He took a neck brush and swept a chair for her. She stared, irresolute.

'Go on. We all feel like that, sometimes. Most of us don't dare. Sit down.'

They all gathered round, the young, making sooth-ing, chirruping noises, putting out hands with vague patting, calming gestures.

'I'll send you a cheque.'

'The insurance'll pay. Don't worry. It's insured. You've done me a good turn in a way. It wasn't quite right, the colours. I might do something different. Or collect the insurance and give up. Me and my girlfriend are thinking of setting up a stall in the Antique Hyper-market. Costume jewellery. Thirties and forties kitsch. She has sources. I can collect the insurance and have a go. I've had enough of this. I'll tell you something, I've often felt like smashing it all up myself, just to get out of it—like a great glass cage it is—and go out into the real world. So you mustn't worry, dear.'

She sat at home and shook, her cheeks flushed, her eyes bright with tears. When she had pulled herself together, she would go and have a shower and soak out the fatal coils, reduce them to streaming rat-tails. Her husband came in, unexpected—she had long given up expecting or not expecting him, his movements were unpredictable and unexplained. He came in tentatively, a large, alert, ostentatiously work-wearied man. She looked up at him speechless. He saw her. (Usually he did not.)

'You look different. You've had your hair done. I like it. You look lovely. It takes twenty years off you. You should have it done more often.'

And he came over and kissed her on the shorn nape of her neck, quite as he used to do.

Art Work

*L'artiste et le modèle reflétés
dans le miroir,* 1937

Art Work

In 1947 Matisse painted *Le Silence habité des maisons*. It is reproduced in Sir Lawrence Gowing's *Matisse*, only very small and in black and white. Two people sit at the corner of a table. The mother, it may be, has a reflective chin propped on a hand propped on the table. The child, it may be, turns the page of a huge white book, whose arch of paper makes an integral curve with his/her lower arm. In front, a vase of flowers. Behind, six huge panes of window, behind them, a mass of trees and perhaps sunlight. The people's faces are perfect blank ovals, featureless. Up above them, in the top lefthand corner of the canvas, level with the top of the window, is a chalked outline, done as it might be by a child, of a round on a stalk, above bricks. It is a pity there are no colours but it is possible, tempting, to imagine them, sumptuous as they were in what Gowing says was 'the reconciliation which is only within the reach of great painters in old age'. The pictures, Gowing says, have extraordinary virility. 'At last Matisse is wholly at ease with the fierce impulse.' It is a dark little image on the page, charcoal-grey, slate-grey, soft pale pencil-grey, subdued, demure. We may imagine it flaming, in carmine or vermilion, or swaying in indigo darkness, or perhaps—outdoors—gold and green. We may imagine it. The darkness of the child may be black on black or black on blue or blue on some sort of red. The book is white. Who is the watching totem under the ceiling?

There is an inhabited silence in 49 Alma Road, in the sense that there are no voices, though there are various sounds, some of them even pervasive and raucous sounds, which an unconcerned ear might construe as the background din of a sort of silence. There is the churning hum of the washing-machine, a kind of splashy mechanical giggle, with a grinding note in it, tossing its wet mass one way, resting and simmering, tossing it the other. A real habitué of this noise will tense him or herself against the coming banshee-scream of the spin-cycle, accompanied by a drumming tattoo of machine feet scrabbling on the tiles.

The dryer is chuntering too. It is not a new dryer, its carbon brushes are worn, it thumps and creaks and screeches in its slow circling. The mass of cloth inside it flails, flops with a crash, rises, flails, flops with a crash. An attentive ear could hear the difference in the texture and mass of the flop as the sleeves and stockings are bound into sausages and balls by the fine straps of petticoats and bras.

In the front room, chanting to itself, for no one is watching it, the television is full on in mid-morning. Not loudly, there are rules about noise. The noise it is making is the wilfully upbeat cheery squitter of female presenters of children's TV, accented with regular, repetitive amazement, mixed in with the grunts and cackles and high-pitched squeaks of a flock of furry puppets, a cross-eyed magenta haystack with a snout, a kingfisher blue gerbil with a whirling tail, a torpid emerald green coiled serpent, with a pillar-box red dangling tongue and movable fringed eyelids. At regular intervals, between the bouts of presenter-squitter and puppet snorts and squawks, comes, analogous to the spin-cycle, the musical outbursts, a drumroll, a squeal on a wood-wind, a percussion battery, a ta-ta ta TA, for punctuation, for a roseate full-frame with a lime-coloured logo T-NE-TV.

On the first floor, behind a closed door, the circular rush and swish of Jamie's electric trains can be heard. Nothing can be heard of Natasha's record-player, and Natasha cannot hear the outside world, for her whole head is stuffed with beating vibrations and exploding howls and ululations. She lies on her bed and twitches in rhythm. Anyone coming in could well hear, from the other side of the corridor, the twangling tinny bumps made by the baffled sound trying to break out of its boxer-glove packaging. Natasha's face has the empty beatific intelligence of some of Matisse's supine women. Her face is white and oval and luminous with youth. Her hair is inky blue-black, and fanned across her not-too-clean pillows. Her bedspread is jazzy black forms of ferns or seaweeds, on a scarlet ground, forms the textile designer would never have seen, without Matisse. Her arms and legs dangle beyond the confines of the ruffled rectangle of this spread, too gawky to be an odalisque, but just as delicious in their curves. White, limp, relaxed, twitching. Twitches can't be painted.

From Debbie's room comes the sound of the type-writer. It is an old mechanical typewriter, its noises are metallic and clicking. It chitters on to the end of a line, then there is the clash of the return, and the musical, or almost musical 'cling' of the little bell. Tap tap tap tap tappety tappety tappety clash cling tappety tap tap. A silence. Debbie sits over her typewriter with her oval chin in her long hands, and her black hair coiled gracefully in her neck. It is easy to see where Natasha's ink and ivory beauty comes from. Debbie frowns. She taps a tooth (ivory lacquer, a shade darker than the skin) with an oval nail, rose madder. Debbie's office, or study, is very cramped. There is a drawing-board, but if it is not in use, it is blocked up against the window, obscuring much of the light, and all of the vision of pillar-box red geraniums and cobalt-blue lobelias in a window box on the sill. Debbie can work at her desk or work at her drawing-board, but not both at once, though she would like to be able to, she is the design editor of *A Woman's Place,* of which the, perhaps obscure, premise is that a woman's place is not only, perhaps not even primarily, in the Home. Debbie is working at home at the moment because Jamie has chicken pox and the doctor is coming, and the doctor cannot say at what time he will or won't call, there is too much pressure. Jamie has the same inky hair as his mother and sister, and has even longer blacker lashes over black eyes. He has the same skin too, but at the moment it is a wonderfully humped and varied terrain of rosy peaks and hummocks, mostly the pink of those boring little begonias with fleshy leaves, but some raging into salmon-deeps and some extinct volcanoes, with umber and ochre crusts. It was Jamie who was watching the TV but he cannot stick at anything, he itches too wildly, he tears at his flesh with his bitten-down nails, he rubs himself against chairs. Debbie stood him on a coffee table and swabbed and painted him with calamine lotion, creating a kind of streaked sugar or plaster of Paris mannikin, with powdery pinky-beige crude surfaces, rough make-up, failed paint, a dull bland colour, under which the bumpy buds of the pox heated themselves into re-emergence. 'War-paint,' Debbie said to her son, squeezing and stippling the liquid on his round little belly, between his poor hot legs. 'You could put stripes of cocoa on,' said Jamie. 'And icing sugar. That would make three colours of stripes.' Debbie would have liked to paint him all over, with fern-green cake dye and cochineal, if that would have distracted or assuaged him, but she had to get the piece she was writing done, which was about the new wave of kitchen plastic design, wacky colours, staggering new stream-lined shapes.

On Debbie's walls, which are lemon-coloured, are photographs of Natasha and Jamie as naked babies, and later, gap-toothed, grinning school heads and shoulders, a series of very small woodcuts, illustrating fairy tales, a mermaid, an old witch with a spindle, a bear and two roses, and in a quite different style a small painting of a table, a hyper-realist wooden table with a blue vase and a small Rubik's cube on it. Also, in white frames, two paintings done by a younger Natasha, a vase of anemones, watery crimsons and purples, a dress flung over a chair, blue dress, grey chair, promising folds, in a probably unintentional void.

Debbie types, and cocks her head for the sound of the doorbell. She types 'a peculiarly luscious new purple, like bilberry juice with a little cream swirled in it'. She jumps at the sound not of the doorbell but of her telephone, one of the new fluttering burrs, disconcertingly high-pitched. It is her editor, asking when she will be able to make a layout conference. She speaks, placating, explaining, just sketching in an appeal for sympathy. The editor of *A Woman's Place* is a man, who reads and slightly despises the pieces about the guilt of the working mother which his periodical periodically puts out. Debbie changes tack, and makes him laugh with a description of where poor Jamie's spots have managed to sprout. 'Poor little bugger,' quacks the editor into Debbie's ear, inaudible to the rest of the house.

Up and down the stairs, joining all three floors, surges a roaring and wheezing noise, a rhythmic and complex and swelling crescendo, snorting, sucking, with a high-pitched drone planing over a kind of grinding sound, interrupted every now and then by a frenetic rattle, accompanied by a new, menacing whine. Behind the Hoover, upwards and downwards, comes Mrs Brown, without whom, it must immediately be said, Debbie's world would not hold together.

Mrs Brown came ten years ago, in answer to an advertisement in the local paper. Natasha was four, and Jamie

was on the way. Debbie was unwell and at her wits' end,
with fear of losing her job. She put 'artistic family' in the
advertisement, expecting perhaps to evoke some toler-
ance, if not positive affection, for the tattered wallpaper
and burgeoning mess. She didn't have much response—
a couple of art students, one an unmarried mum who
wanted to share babysitting, painting-time, and chores,
a very old, purblind, tortoise-paced ex-parlourmaid,
and Mrs Brown. Mrs Brown had a skin which was neither black nor brown but a kind of amber yellow, the
sort of yellow bruises go, before they vanish, but all
over. She had a lot of wiry soot-coloured hair, which
rose, like the crown of a playing-card king, out of a ban-
deau of flowery material, tied tightly about her brow,
like the towelling of a tennis star, or the lace cap of an
oldfashioned maid. Mrs Brown's clothes were, and are,
flowery and surprising, jumble sale remnants, rejects
and ends of lines, rainbow-coloured jumpers made from
the ping-pong-ball-sized unwanted residues of other
people's knitting. She came for her interview in a not
too clean (but not too dirty) film-star's trench-coat,
which she didn't take off until Debbie had said, dry-
mouthed with anxiety, 'I think you and I might manage

to get on, don't you?' And Mrs Brown had nodded deci-
sively, accepted a cup of coffee, and divested herself of
the trench-coat, revealing pantaloons made of some
kind of thick cream-coloured upholstery linen, wonderfully traversed by crimson open-mouthed Indian flowers and birds of paradise and tendrils of unearthly
creepers, and a royal-blue jumper embroidered all over
with woollen daisies, white marguerites, orange black-
eyed Susans.

Mrs Brown does not smile very much. Her face has
some resemblance to a primitive mask, cheeks in triangular planes, long, straight, salient nose, a mouth usually tightly closed. Her expression can be read as prim,
or grim, or watchful or perhaps—though this is not the
first idea that comes to mind—perhaps resigned. She
likes to go barefoot in the house, it turns out—she is not
used to this level of heating, she explains, implying—or
does Debbie misread her?—that the heating is an un-
healthy extravagance. She comes up behind you with no
warning, and at first this used to irritate Debbie most
frightfully, but now she is used to it, she is used to Mrs
Brown, her most powerful emotion in relation to Mrs
Brown is terror that she will leave. If Mrs Brown is not

Debbie's friend, she is the closest person to Debbie on earth, excluding perhaps the immediate family. Debbie and Mrs Brown do not share the usual intimacies, they have no common chatter about other people, but they have a kind of rock-bottom knowledge of each other's fears and pains, or so Debbie thinks, knowing, nevertheless, that Mrs Brown knows more about her than she will ever know about Mrs Brown, since it is in Debbie's house that the relationship is carried out. Mrs Brown washes Debbie's underwear and tidies Debbie's desk, putting Debbie's letters, private and official, threatening and secret, in tidy heaps. Mrs Brown counts the bottles and sweeps up the broken glass after parties, though she does not partake of the festive food. Mrs Brown changes Debbie's sheets.

Debbie did not ask Mrs Brown at that decisive interview whether Mrs Brown had children, though she was dying to, because she, Debbie, so resents being asked, by those interviewing her for jobs, whether she has children, what she would do with them. She did ask if Mrs Brown had a telephone, and Mrs Brown said yes, she did, she found it essential, she used the word 'essential' tidily and drily, just like that, without elaboration. 'So you will tell me in advance, if at all possible,' says Debbie, trying to sound sweet and commonly courteous, 'if you can't come ever, if you aren't going to be able to come ever, because I have to make such complicated arrangements if people are going to let me down, that is, can't make it for any reason.' 'I think you'll find I'm reliable,' says Mrs Brown. 'But it's no good me saying so, you'll have to see. You needn't worry though, bar the unforeseen.' 'Acts of God,' says Debbie. 'Well, and acts of Hooker too,' says Mrs Brown, without saying who Hooker might be.

Debbie did find that Mrs Brown was, as she had said, reliable. She also discovered, not immediately, that Mrs Brown had two sons, Lawrence and Gareth, shortened to Gary by his friends but not by Mrs Brown. These boys were already ten and eight when Mrs Brown came to Debbie. Lawrence is now at Newcastle University—'the lodgings are cheaper up there' says Mrs Brown. Gareth has left home without many qualifications and works, Mrs Brown says, 'in distribution'. He has made the wrong sort of friends, Mrs Brown says, but does not elaborate. Hooker is the father of Lawrence and Gareth. Debbie does not know, and does not ask, whether

Hooker is or is not Mr Brown. During the early childhood of Natasha and Jamie, Hooker would make sudden forays into Mrs Brown's life and council flat, from which he had departed before she took to going out to clean up after people like Debbie. One of Mrs Brown's rare days off was her court appearance to get an injunction to stop Hooker coming round. Hooker was the cause of Mrs Brown's bruises, the chocolate and violet stains on the gold skin, the bloody cushions in the hair and the wine-coloured efflorescence on her lips. Once, and once only, at this time, Debbie found Mrs Brown sitting on the bathroom stool, howling, and brought her cups of coffee, and held her hands, and sent her home in a taxi. It was Mrs Brown who saw Debbie through the depression after the birth of Jamie, with a mixture of carefully timed indulgences and requirements. 'I've brought you a bowl of soup, you'll do no good in the world if you don't eat.' 'I've brought Baby up to you, Mrs Dennison, he's crying his heart out with hunger, he needs his mother, that's what it is.' They call each other Mrs Dennison and Mrs Brown. They rely on the kind of distance and breathing space this courtesy gives them. Mrs Brown was scathing about the days in hospital, when she was concussed, after one of Hooker's visits. 'They call you love, and dearie, and pet. I say, I need a bit of respect, my name is Mrs Brown.'

Debbie types 'new moulding techniques give new streamlined shapes to the most banal objects. Sink trays and storage jars . . .' Banal is the wrong word, she thinks. Everyday? Wrong too. The Hoover snorts on the turning of the stair. The doorbell rings. A voice of pure male rage rings out from the top floor.

'Debbie. Debbie, are you there? Just come here a moment.'

Debbie is torn. Mrs Brown abandons the Hoover and all its slack, defunct-seeming tubes, along the banisters.

'You attend to *him*, and I'll just let the doctor in and say you'll be down directly.'

Debbie negotiates the Hoover and goes up the attic stairs.

'Look,' says Debbie's husband, Robin. 'Look what she has done. If you can't get it into her head that she mustn't muck about with my work-things she'll have to go.'

Robin has the whole third floor, once three bedrooms,

a tiny room with a sink and a lavatory, as his studio. He has large pivoting windows set into the roof, with linen blinds, a natural cream, a terracotta. He can have almost whatever light he likes from whatever angle. Debbie feels her usual knot of emotions, fear that Robin will shout at Mrs Brown, fear that Mrs Brown will take offence, rage and grim gratitude mixed that it is always to her that he addresses his complaints.

'The doctor has come for Jamie, darling,' Debbie says. 'I must go, he won't have long.'

'This bowl,' says Robin Dennison, 'this bowl, as anyone can see, is a work of art. Look at that glaze. Look at those huge satisfactory blue and orange fruits in it, look at the green leaves and the bits of yellow, just *look*, Debbie. Now I ask you, would anyone suppose this bowl was a kind of *dustbin* for things they were too lazy to put away or carry off, would they, do you suppose, anyone *with their wits about them*, would they?'

'What's the matter?' says Debbie neutrally, her ear turned to the stairs.

'*Look*,' cries Robin. The bowl, both sumptuously decorated and dusty, contains a few random elastic bands, a chain of paperclips, an obscure plastic cog from some tiny clock, a battered but unused stamp, two oil pastels, blue and orange, a piece of dried bread, a very short length of electric wire, a dead chrysanthemum, three coloured thumbtacks (red, blue, green), a single lapis cufflink, an electric bulb with a burnt patch on its curve, a box of matches, a china keyhole cover, two indiarubbers, a dead bluebottle and two live ants, running in circles, possibly busy, possibly frantically lost.

'Her habits are filthy,' says Robin.

Debbie looks around the studio, which is not the habitation of a tidy man. Apart from the inevitable mess, splashed palettes, drying canvases, jars of water, there are other heaps and dumps. Magazines, opened and closed, wineglasses, beer glasses, bottles, constellations of crayons and pencils, unopened messages from the Income Tax, saucers of clips and pins.

'It is hard for anyone to tell what to leave alone, up here, and what to clear up.'

'No, it isn't. Dirt is dirt, and personal *things*, things in use, are things in use. All it requires is intelligence.'

'She seems to have found that cufflink you were going on about.'

'I expect I found it myself, and put it down some-where safe, and she interfered with it.'

All this is part of a ritual dialogue which Debbie can hardly bear to hear again, let alone to utter her own banal parts of it, and yet she senses it is somehow necessary to their survival. She does not wholly know whether it is necessary because Robin needs to assert himself and win, or because if she does not stand between Robin and Mrs Brown Mrs Brown will leave. She does not need to think about it any more; she turns and hearkens to it, like Donne's other compass half, like a heliotrope.

'She could see I was painting *exactly* that dish.'

Indeed, there are sketches in charcoal, in coloured chalks, of exactly that dish, on an expanse of grained wood, propped up around the studio.

It crosses Debbie's mind that Mrs Brown used exactly that dish as a picking-up receptacle for exactly that reason. Mrs Brown has her own modes of silent aggression. She does not raise this idea. Robin is neither moved by nor interested in Mrs Brown's feelings.

'Shall I take them all and throw them away in the bin in my study, darling? And dust your bowl for you?'

'Wait a minute. Those are quite all right rubber bands. I was using that bread for rubbing out. The matches are OK, nothing wrong with them. Some of us can't afford to throw good tools away, you know.'

'Where shall I put them?'

'Just stick them on the table over there. I'll see to them myself. Dust the bowl, please.'

Debbie does as he asks, abstracting the cufflink, which she will return to his dressing-table. She looks at her husband, who glares back at her, and then gives a smile, like a rueful boy. He is a long, thin, unsubstantial man in jeans and a fisherman's smock, with big joints, knuckles and wrists and ankles, like an adolescent, which he is not. He has a very English face, long and fine and pink and white, like a worried colt. His soft hair is pushed up all round his head like a hedgehog and is more or less the same colour as one. His eyes are an intense blue, like speedwells. A photographer could choose between making him look like a gentle mystic and making him look like a dedicated cricketer. A painter could choose between a haziness at the edges, always light, never heavy, and very clear sketched-in features, bones, a brow, a chin, a clearcut nose, in a kind of pale space.

'You *have* managed to make her understand about the fetishes.'

'It took long enough,' he grumbles. 'I even gave her lectures on tones and complementary colours, I just *stood* there with the things and showed her.'

'I should think that was interesting for her.'

'She should know her job, without all that fuss. Anyway, it worked, I grant you that it worked.'

'I must go, darling, the doctor's here. Do you want coffee when he's gone, shall I bring you a mug?'

'Yes please. That will be nice.'

He is not apologising, but the ritual confrontation is over. Debbie kisses him. His cheek is soft. She says,

'Have you heard from that girl from the Callisto Gallery, yet?'

'I don't think she'll come. I don't think she ever meant to come.'

'Yes, she did,' said Debbie. 'I talked to her, too. She really liked that blue and yellow plate picture Toby has got in his loo. She said she didn't think much of Toby's taste in general, but that was exquisite, she said, she said she just sat there staring at it and caused an awful queue!'

'She was probably drunk.'

'Don't be *silly*, Robin. She'll turn up, I know. I don't say things I don't mean, do I?'

Debbie doesn't know whether the girl, Shona McRury, will turn up or not, but she says she will, with force, because it is better for her, as well as for Robin, if he is in a hopeful mood. Deborah loves Robin. She has loved him since they met at Art School, where she studied Graphic Design and he studied Fine Art. She wanted to be a wood-engraver and illustrate children's books. What she loved about Robin was the quality of his total dedication to his work, which had a certain austere separateness from everyone else's work. Those were the days of the sixties, in fact the early seventies, when much painting was abstract, washes of colour and no colour, geometric patterns, games with the nature of canvas and pigment and the colours of light and their effect on the eye. Robin was a neo-realist before neo-realism. He painted what he saw, metal surfaces, wooden surfaces, plaster surfaces, with hallucinatory skill and accuracy.

He painted expanses of neutral colours—wooden planks, glass table-tops, beige linen, crumbling plaster, and somewhere, somewhere unexpected, not quite in a corner, not quite in the centre, not where the folds were pulling from or the planks ran, he painted something very small and very brilliant, a glass ball, a lustre vase, a bouquet of bone china flowers (never anything alive), a heap of feathers. It was just this side of kitsch, then and now. It could have been turned into sweet prints and sold in folders in gift shops, then, for its wit, now for its nostalgic emptiness containing verisimilitude. But Debbie saw that it was a serious attempt at a serious and terrible problem, an attempt to answer the question every artist must ask him or herself, at some time, why bother, why make representations of anything at all?

She said to him, seeing her first two of the series, a hexagonal Chinese yellow box on a grey blanket, a paperweight on a kitchen table, 'They are miraculous, they are like those times when time seems to stop, and you just *look* at something, and *see* it, out of time, and you feel surprised that you can see at all, you are *so surprised*, and the seeing goes on and on, and gets better and better . . .'

'Is that what you see in them?' he said.

'Oh yes. Isn't that what you meant?'

'It is exactly what I meant. But nobody's ever seen it. Or nobody's ever said it, anyway.'

'I expect they do, really.'

'Sometimes I think, it just looks—ordinary—to other people. *Unprivileged* things, you know.'

'How could it?' said Debbie.

Sex makes everything shine, even if it is not privileged, and Debbie made Robin happy and their happiness made his pictures seem stranger and brighter, perhaps even made them, absolutely, stranger and brighter. When they got married, Robin had a few hours part-time teaching in a college, and Debbie, whose degree gave her more marketable skills, got a job doing layout in a corset-trade magazine, and then a subordinate job in *A Woman's Place*, and then promotion. She was good, she was well-paid, she was the breadwinner. It seemed silly for Robin to go on teaching at all, his contribution was so meagre. Debbie's head was full of snazzy swimsuits and orange vats of carrot soup with emerald parsley sprinkled in it, with lipsticks from grape and plum to poppy and rose, with eyegloss and blusher and the ghosts of unmade woodcuts. Her fingers remembered the slow, careful work in the wood, with a quiet grief, that didn't diminish, but was manageable. She hated Robin because he never once mentioned the unmade wood-engravings. It is possible to feel love and hate quite quietly, side by side, if one is a self-contained person. Debbie continued to love Robin, whilst hating him because of the woodcuts, because of the extent of his absence of interest in how she managed the house, the children, the money, her profession, his needs and wants, and because of his resolute attempts to unsettle, humiliate, or drive away Mrs Brown, without whom all Debbie's balancing acts would clatter and fall in wounding disarray.

Left to himself, Robin Dennison walks agitated up and down his studio. He is over forty. He thinks, I am over forty. He prevents himself, all the time now, from seeing his enterprise, his work, his life, as absurd. He is not suited to the artistic life, in most ways. By upbringing and temperament, he should have been a solicitor or an accountant, he should have worn a suit and fished for trout and played cricket. He has no great self-confidence, no braggadocio, no real or absolute disposition to the sort of self-centred isolation he practises. He does it out of a stubborn faithfulness to a vision he had, a long time ago now, a vision which has never expanded or diminished or taken its teeth out of him. He was given a set of gouache paints by an aunt when he was a boy, and painted a geranium, and then a fish-tank. He can still remember the illicit, it seemed to him, burst out of sensuous delight with which he saw the wet carmine trail of his first flick of the brush, the slow circling of the wet hairs in a cobalt pool, the dashes of yellow ochre and orange, as he conjured up, on matt white, wet and sinuous fish-tails and fins. He was not much good at anything else, which muted any familial conflict over his choice of future. With his brushes in his hand he could *see*, he told himself, through art school. Without them, he was grey fog in a world of grey fog. He painted small bright things in large expanses of grey and buff and beige. Everyone said, 'He's *got* something,' or more dubiously, 'He's got *something*.' Probably not enough, they qualified this, silently to themselves, but Robin heard them well enough, for all that.

He could talk to Debbie. Debbie knew about his vision of colour, he had told her, and she had listened. He talked to her agitatedly at night about Matisse, about the paradoxical way in which the pure sensuousness of *Luxe, calme et volupté* could be a religious experience of the nature of things. Not softness, he said to Debbie, *power,* calm power.

Debbie said yes, she understood, and they went to the South of France for a holiday, to be in the strong light, là-bas. This was a disaster. He tried putting great washes of strong colour on the canvas, à la Matisse, à la Van Gogh, and it came out watery and feeble and absurd, there was nothing he could do. His only successful picture of that time was a kind of red beetle or bug and a large shining green-black scarab and a sulphurous butterfly on a seat of pebbles, grey and pinkish and sandy and buff and white and terracotta, you can imagine the kind of thing, it is everywhere in all countries, a variegated expanse of muted pebbles. Extending to all the four corners of the world of the canvas, a stony desert, with a dead leaf or two, and some random straws, and the baleful insects. He sold that one to a gallery and had hopes, but heard no more, his career did not take off, and they never went back to the strong light, they take their holidays in the Cotswolds.

Robin has ritualised his life dangerously, but this is not, as he thinks it is, entirely because of his precarious vocation. His father, a Borough Surveyor, behaved in much the same way, particularly with regard to his distinction between his own untouchable 'things' and other people's, especially the cleaning-lady's 'filth'. Mr Dennison, Mr Rodney Dennison, used to shout at and about the 'charwoman' if pipe-dottle was thrown away, or soap-fragments amalgamated, or scattered bills tidily gathered. He, like Robin with Mrs Brown, used to feel a kind of panic of constriction, like the pain of sinus-fluid thickening in the skull-pockets, when threatened by tidy touches. He, like Robin, used to see Mrs Briggs's progress like a snail-trail across his private spaces. Robin puts it all down to Art. He does not ask himself if his hatred of Mrs Brown is a deflected resentment of his helplessness in the capable hands of his wife, breadwinner and life-manager. He knows it is not so: Debbie is beautiful and clean and represents order. Mrs Brown is chaotic and wild to look at and a secret smoker and represents— even while dispersing or re-distributing it—'filth'.

Mrs Brown has always had an awkward habit of presuming to give the family gifts. She possesses a knitting-machine, which Hooker got off the back of a lorry, and she is also good with knitting needles, crochet-hooks, embroidery silks and tapestry (not often, these two last, they are too expensive). She makes all her own clothes, out of whatever comes to hand, old plush curtains, Arab blankets, parachute silk, his own discarded trousers. She makes them flamboyantly, with patches and fringes and braid and bizarre buttons. The epitome of tat, Robin considers, and he has to consider, for she always strikes the eye, in a magenta and vermilion overall over salmon-pink crêpe pantaloons, in a lime-green shift with black lacy inserts. This would not be so bad, if she didn't make, hadn't made for years, awful jumpers for Natasha and Jamie, awful rainbow jumpers in screaming hues, candy-striped jumpers, jumpers with bobble-cherries bouncing on them, long peculiar rainbow scarves in fluffy angora, all sickly ice-cream colours. Robin tells Debbie these things must be sent back *at once*, his children can't be seen *dead* in them. The children are ambivalent, depending on age and circumstances. Jamie wore out one jumper with red engines and blue cows when he was six and would not be parted from it. Natasha in her early teens had an unexpected success at a disco in a kind of dayglo fringed bolero (acid yellow, salmon pink, swimming-pool blue) but has rejected other offerings with her father's fastidious distaste. The real sufferer is Debbie, whose imagination is torn all ways. She knows from her own childhood exactly how it feels to wear clothes one doesn't like, isn't comfortable and invisible in, is embarrassed by. She also believes very strongly that there is more true kindness and courtesy in accepting gifts gratefully and enthusiastically than in making them. And, more selfishly, she simply cannot do without Mrs Brown, she needs Mrs Brown, her breakfast table is ornamented with patchwork tea-cosies contributed by Mrs Brown, her study chairs have circular cushions knitted in sugar-pink and orange by Mrs Brown. Mrs Brown stands in Debbie's study door sometimes and expounds her colour theory.

'They always told us, didn't they, the teachers and grans, orange and pink, they make you blink, blue and green should not be seen, mauve and red cannot be wed, but I say, they're all there, the colours, God made 'em all, and mixes 'em all in His creatures, what exists goes together somehow or other, don't you think, Mrs Dennison?'

'Well, yes, but there are rules too, you know, Mrs Brown, how to get certain effects, there are *rules,* complementary colours and things . . .'

'I'm learning all that. *He* tells me, when I move his things by accident, or whatever. Fascinating.'

Mrs Brown's yellow face is long, unsmiling and judicious. She adds, 'If Jamie's got no use for that nice sky-blue tank-top I did for him I'll have it back if you don't mind, I've got a use for a bit of sky-blue.'

'Oh, he *loves* it, Mrs Brown, it's just a wee bit tight under the armpits, you understand . . .'

'As I said, I've got a use for a bit of sky-blue.'

Implacably. Debbie feels terrible. Mrs Brown goes through Jamie's drawers and points out that there are holes in his red sweat-shirt, that those rugger socks are shockingly shrunk, look at those tiddly feet. She puts them in a plastic dustbin bag. Debbie adds a cocktail dress she made a mistake about, mulberry shot silk, and two of Robin's ties, presents from his auntie Nem, which he will never wear, because they are a horrible mustard colour with plummy flowers.

'Interesting,' says Mrs Brown, holding them up like captured eels, and adding them to her spoils. She is mol-

lified, Debbie thinks, the mulberry dress has mollified her. She balks at knowing what Mrs Brown will do with the mulberry dress.

Robin Dennison's 'fetishes' have a table of their own, a white-painted wooden table, very simple. Once they were mantelpiece 'things' but as they took on their status of 'fetishes' they were given this solidly unassuming English altar. What they have in common is a certain kind of glossy, very brightly coloured solidity. They are the small icons of a cult of colour. They began with the soldier, who cost 5/6 when Robin was little, and is made of painted wood, with red trousers and a blue jacket and a tall, bulbous, black wooden bearskin. His red is fading cherry-crimson, his blue is a fading colour between royal and ultramarine. He has a gold strap under his wooden chin and a pair of hectic pink circular spots on his wooden cheeks. Robin does not often paint him now—he cannot clear him of his double connotations of militarism and infantilism, and he loves him for neither of these, but because he was his first model for slivers of shine on rounded surfaces. Sometimes Robin paints his *shadow* into little crowds of the other things.

Some of the other things are pure representations of single colours. Of these, two are gloss—a cobalt-blue candlestick from the glassworks at Biot, and a round heavy grass-green, golden-green apple made by Wedgwood, greener and greener in its depths. The yellow thing was much the most expensive. It is not pure yellow as the candlestick is blue, and the apple is green, it is sunny-yellow, butter-yellow, buttercup-yellow with a blue rim, a reproduction sauceboat from Monet's self-designed breakfast service for his house at Giverny. It cost £50 which Robin did not have, but spent, he wanted *that* yellow so much. He did not really want the sauce-boat, but anything else he wanted cost money which even in his madness he saw he didn't have. Robin in his fit of educating Mrs Brown observes to her that the blue rim makes the yellow colour sing out because the colours are almost complementary. He would, however, still like to find a yellow thing without the blue. There is no orange thing either. Robin often stands an orange and a lemon amongst the things, to make the colours complete, and Mrs Brown's habit of moving these, or even throwing them away when they begin to soften and darken and grow patches of sage-green, blue-specked mould, is one of the things that makes Robin see red and roar.

Purple is represented by a rather sweet hand-made china sculpture of a round bowl of violets. These are both pale mauve and deep purple; they have a few, not many, green leaves in a wishy-washy apple colour, and their container is a softly-glazed black. Sometimes Robin leaves the leaves out, when he doesn't want that colour. He knows the fetishes so well, he can allow for the effect of the leaves on the violets. Sometimes he wishes the leaves weren't there and sometimes he *makes* them fit into his colour-scheme with delicate shifts of tones and accommodations in other places. There was a problem with red for years and years. There was a banal red German plate, modern and utilitarian, a good strong red, that stood in, but could not make itself sing out or be loved. When Robin found the present red thing he felt very uneasy because he knew immediately it was the, or a, *right thing,* and at the same time he didn't like it. He still doesn't. Like the poor soldier, but in more sinister ways, it has too much meaning. He found it in a Chinese bric-à-brac shop, in a dump-bin with hundreds of others. It is a large red, heart-shaped pincushion, plumply and gleamingly covered in a poppy-red silk which is *exactly* what he wants, at once soft and shining, delicate and glossy. It had a vulgar white lace frill, like a choir-boy's collar, which Robin took off. Sometimes he puts into it some of his grandmother's old hatpins, imitation jewels, or lumps of jet. But he doesn't quite like this, it borders on the surrealist, and though he senses that *might* be interesting, it also worries him. He did buy a box of multi-coloured glass-headed pins which he occasionally displays in a random scattering shape, or, once, a tight half-moon.

Besides the single-coloured things, there are a few, a very few, multi-coloured things. A 1950s Venetian glass tree, picked up in a second-hand shop, bearing little round fruits of many colours—emerald green, ruby and dark sapphire, amethyst and topaz. A pottery jug from Deruta with a huge triangular beak-like spout, covered with bright round-petalled childish flowers in all the colours, and a pair of chirpy primitive singing-birds, in brown. A pot, also from Deruta, with a tawny-gold and blue-crested grotesque merman, or human-headed dragon, bearded and breathing a comma-shaped cloud of russet fire. There is a kite on the wall, a Korean kite in puce and yellow and blue and green and scarlet, and there are two large Chinese silk pipe-cleaner birds, crested and flaunting long tails, one predominantly crimson, with a yellow and aquamarine crest, one blue and green. The birds, too, the most fragile things, are a point of contention between Robin and Mrs Brown. She says they collect dust. He says she bends their legs and squashes their down and interferes with the way they turn their necks to preen. She says, they don't balance, the way he fixes them. Once she balanced one on the bough of the glass tree. There was a sulk that lasted weeks, and Mrs Brown talked of leaving.

It was after Debbie patched up this difference that Robin explained to Mrs Brown about red and green. He moved the apple back next to the pincushion, and redeployed the violets in front of the Monet sauceboat, beside the cobalt-blue candlestick, which was shaped a little like a gentian, a tall cup on a stem. Mrs Brown's preference was for standing the fetishes in a rainbow line, from infra-red to ultra-violet, so to speak. Robin said,

'Certain combinations have certain effects. For in-

stance the opposition of yellow and violet, blue and orange, that can appear *natural* in a way, because natural
shadows are blue or violet. Light and shade, you see?
Whereas red and green, if you put them next to each
other—sometimes you can see a kind of dancing yellow
line where they meet—and this isn't to do with light and
shade, it's to do, possibly, with the fact that if you *add*
certain reds to certain greens you can *make* yellow,
which you would never have guessed.'

'Geraniums are natural,' said Mrs Brown.

Robin stared at her abstractedly.

'Natural red and green. They don't make yellow.'

'*Look,*' said Robin, pushing together the soft heart
and the hard apple. He could see the dance of unreal yellow. He was entranced.

'Hmn,' said Mrs Brown.

'Can you see yellow?'

'Well, a sort of, how shall I say, a sort of wriggling, a
sort of shimmering. I see what you mean.'

'I try to make that happen, in the paintings.'

'So I see. It's interesting, once I know what you're
up to.'

The sentence was a concession, unsmiling, not wholly

gracious. She accepted that he had given her what he could, the battle was, she obviously considered, won, and by her. Robin was relieved, really. He was not so far out of touch with real life that he could not sense Debbie's fear of losing Mrs Brown. So he had given Mrs Brown his secret vision of the yellow line. Mrs Brown went out, head high. She was wearing a kind of orange and green camouflage Afro-wrapper, and a pink headband.

Shona McRury telephones. She asks to speak to Debbie, who has in fact answered the phone, and spends a long time congratulating Debbie on an article on feminist art in *A Woman's Place*, an article about the amorphous things that women make that do not claim the 'authority' of 'art-works', the undignified things women 'frame' that male artists have never noticed, tampons and nappies but not only those, and the painted interior cavities of women, not the soft fleshy desirable superficies explored/exploited by men. Debbie has made a lovely centre-spread of the crayon drawings of an artist called Brenda Murphy, who works in the kitchen with her children, using *their* materials, crayons and felt-tips on paper, creating works that are a savage and loving commentary on their lives together. Shona asks Debbie if she knows if Ms Murphy has an agent or a gallery, and Debbie answers abstractedly, praises the interesting variety, the eclectic brilliance of Callisto's shows, and is rewarded by Shona McRury's request to see Debbie's husband's work, which is so *witty,* she thinks, she just loves that mysteriously funny little painting in Toby's loo, a jewel in a desert. Debbie thinks a jewel in a desert is a good phrase, but is not sure the idea of *wit* bodes well. Robin is, she recognises, somewhat humourless in his driven state. But she fixes something exact, for this coming Wednesday, without consulting Robin. Robin is perturbed and threatened by the closeness of Wednesday, as Debbie has foreseen. She becomes ever so slightly minatory, and at the same time plaintive. 'It isn't so easy to get a chance of getting the work seen by a gallery, you can't just pick and choose your moments or you end up with *none,* as you ought to know by now, and I've done my best for you, I pinned her down, you have to, she's so busy, even with the best will in the world . . .'

Robin condescends, in terror, to have his work viewed.

Shona McRury has topaz eyes and long, silky brown hair, like a huge ribbon, caught up at the back with a tortoiseshell comb. She wears topaz ear-rings, little spheres on gold chains, that exactly match her eyes, and an olive silk suit, with a loose jacket and a pleated skirt, over a lemon-yellow silk shirt, all of which tone in impeccably with her eyes. (Debbie who is now a professional in these matters sees immediately how the whole delicate and powerful effect is constructed around the eyes, reinforced by a subtle powdering of olive and gold shadow shot with a sharper green, almost malachite.) She climbs up to Robin's attic on dark-green lizard-skin shoes. Between the lizard skin and the olive silk are slightly golden metallic stockings on legs not quite beautiful, too thin, too straight. Robin goes first, then Shona McRury, then Debbie, then Mrs Brown, with a bottle of chilled Sauvignon and three glasses on a Japanese lacquer tray. Mrs Brown is wearing her bird-of-paradise upholstery trousers and a patchwork shirt in rainbow colours, stitched together with red feather-stitching. Although she has not brought herself a glass, she positions herself inside the studio door for the showing, and makes no attempt to go away, staring with sombre interest at Shona McRury's elegance and Robin's canvases.

Debbie has not decided whether to leave Robin alone with Shona McRury, or to stay and put in a word here and there. Mrs Brown's odd behaviour decides her, and is perhaps altogether too decisive. It is not in Debbie's power to say anything like, 'You may go now, Mrs Brown,' but she can say to her, 'Come on, let's leave them to it,' so she does, and she and Mrs Brown go downstairs together.

Shona McRury prowls in Robin's studio in her topaz ear-rings and lizard shoes. She rearranges the fetishes absentmindedly, rattling the Monet dish in its saucer. Robin puts up a series of paintings of the fetishes on different backgrounds, in different numbers, in different lights. White silk like a glacier, crumpled newspaper, dark boards, pale boards. Her mouth is large and soft and brown. She lights a cigarette. She says, 'I *like* that,' and 'I *like* that,' and nothing else for a bit, and then begins to read the paintings as allegories. 'They're modern *vanitas*es, I see,' says Shona McRury, 'they're about the *littleness* of our life.' Robin tries to keep quiet. He cannot overbear her as if she were Mrs Brown, he cannot tell her that they are not about littleness but about the infinite terror of the brilliance of colour, of which he could almost die, he doesn't think those things in words anyway. He does at first say things like, 'Hmn, well, this one is solving a different kind of problem, d'you see?' and then he doesn't say anything because he can see she doesn't see, she isn't the slightest bit interested in the fact that the pictures, of which there are a very large number, never repeat, though they are all in a sense the same, they never set themselves exactly the same problem. She doesn't see that. She says, 'It's a bit frightening, a bit depressing, all that empty space, isn't it, it reminds you of coffins and bare kitchen tables with no food, no sustenance, all those bare boards, don't they?'

'I don't think of it that way,' says Robin.

'How do you think of it?'

'Well, as a series of problems, really, inexhaustible problems, of light and colour, you know.'

He does not say, because he does not articulate, the sense he has that he is *allowed* his patch of brilliance *be-*

cause he has dutifully and accurately and even beautifully painted all these null and neutral tones, the doves, the dusts, the dead leaves.

'Do you have any inkling of a change of direction, a next phase coming up, you know, a new focus of interest, anything like that?'

'I think if I had a big show—if it were all on *show together*, all the different—hm—aspects—hm—solutions, so to speak, temporary solutions—I might want to—move on to something else. It's hard to imagine, really.'

'Is it?'

He does not see how crucial this little question is. 'Oh yes. One thing at a time. I seem to have my work cut out, cut out, you know, for me, as it were, yes.'

Shona McRury says, 'All those prints of lonely deckchairs in little winds, in gardens and on beaches. When you see the first, you think, how moving, how interesting. And when you see the tenth, or the twentieth, you think, oh, *another* solitary deckchair with a bit of wind in it, what else is there? You know?'

'I think so.'

'I can see your work isn't like that.'

'Oh no. Not at all like that.'
'But it might look like that. To the uneducated eye.'
'Might it?'
'It might.'

Debbie watches Shona McRury walk away down Alma Road. How beautifully her olive skirt sits on her thin haunches, how perfectly, how expensively, those pleats are coerced to caress. Robin says his talk with her went well, but Debbie thinks nothing of Robin's judgement, and he does not seem seized with hope or vigour. Shona McRury's long straight band of hair flaps and sidles. Mrs Brown, in her trench-coat, catches up with Shona McRury. Mrs Brown's hair stands up like a wiry plant in a pot, inside a coil of plaited scarves, orange and lime. Mrs Brown says something to Shona McRury who varies her pace, turns her head, strokes her head, answers. Mrs Brown says something else. What can Mrs Brown have to say to Shona McRury? Debbie's mind fantastically meditates treason, subversion, sabotage. But Mrs Brown has always been so good, so patient, despite her disdainful *look,* to which she has a right. Mrs Brown could not want to *hurt* Robin? Mrs Brown is in no position to hurt Robin, surely, if she did. Why should Shona McRury listen, more than out of politeness, to anything Mrs Brown has to say? They turn the corner. Debbie feels tears bursting, somewhere inside the flesh of her cheeks, in the ducts round her nose and eyes. She hears Robin's voice on the stairs, saying it is *just like that woman* to go home without removing the wineglasses or wiping up the rings on his desk and drawing table.

Shona McRury sends a gallery postcard to Robin and Debbie jointly, saying that she really *loved* seeing the pictures, which have *real integrity*, and that things are very crowded and confused in the life of her gallery just now. Debbie knows that this means no, and suspects that the kindnesses are for her, Debbie's, possible future usefulness, that is, *A Woman's Place*'s possible future usefulness, to the Callisto Gallery. She does not say that to Robin, whom she is beginning to treat like a backward and stupid child, which worries her, since that is not what he is. And when *A Woman's Place* sends her off a month or two later to the Callisto Gallery with a photographer, a nice-enough on-the-make Liverpudlian called Tom Sprot, to illustrate an article on a new feminist installation, she goes in a friendly enough mood. She is a reasonable woman, she could not have expected more from Shona McRury, and knows it.

Tom Sprot has brilliantined blond hair and baggy tartan trousers. He is very laid-back, very calm. When he gets inside the gallery, which is normally creamy and airy, he says, 'Wow!' and starts rushing about, peering through his lens, with alacrity. The whole space has been transformed into a kind of soft, even squashy, brilliantly coloured Aladdin's Cave. The walls are hung with what seem like huge tapestries, partly knitted, partly made like rag rugs, with shifting streams and islands of colour, which when looked at closely reveal little peering mad embroidered faces, green with blue eyes, black with red eyes, pink with silver eyes. Swaying crocheted cobwebs hang from the ceiling, inhabited by dusky spiders and swarms of sequined blue flies with gauzy wings. These things are brilliantly pretty, but not like a stage set, they are elegant and sinister, there is something horrid about the netted pockets with the heaped blue bodies. The spiders themselves are menaced by phalanxes of feather dusters, all kinds of feathers, a peacock fan, a fluffy nylon cyan-blue and shocking-pink tube, a lime-green and orange palm tree on a golden staff, wound with lamé. The cavern has a crazy kind of resemblance to a lived-in room. Chests of drawers, made of orange boxes covered with patchworks of wallpaper, from vulgar silver roses to William Morris birds, from Regency plum stripes to Laura Ashley pink sprigs, reveal half-open treasure chests with mazy compartments containing crazy collections of things. White bone buttons. Glass stoppers. Chicken bones. Cufflinks, all single. Medicine bottles with lacquered labels, full of iridescent beads and codliver-oil capsules. Pearlised plastic poppet beads and sunflower seeds, dolls' teaspoons and drifts of variegated tealeaves and dead rose-petals. Sugar mice, some half-chewed. String, bright green, waxed red, hairy brown, running from compartment to compartment.

There are pieces of furniture, or creatures, standing about in all this. A large tump, or possibly a giant pouffe, layered in skirts of scarlet and orange, grass-green and emerald, dazzlingly juxtaposed, reveals, if the wools are parted, a circle of twenty or thirty little knitted pink breasts, and above that another of little chocolate-coloured satin ones, a kind of squat Diana of Ephesus without face or hands. A long bolster-like creature might be a thin woman or a kind of lizard or even a piece of the seashore. It is mostly knitted, in rich browns and greens, with scalloped fronds and trailing, weedy 'limbs' or maybe tentacles—there are more, when it has been walked round, than four. From a distance it has a pleasing look of rock-pools crusted with limpets and anemones. Closer, it can be seen to be plated with a kind of armour of crocheted bosses, violet and saffron, some tufted with crimson, or trailing threads of blood-coloured embroidery-silks.

The centrepiece is a kind of dragon and chained lady, St George and the Princess Saba. Perseus and Andromeda. The dragon has a cubic blue body and a long concertina neck. It has a crest of mulberry taffeta plates, blanket-stitched, something like the horrent scallops of the Stegosaurus. It is an odd dragon, recumbent amongst its own coils, a dragon related to a millipede, with hundreds of black shining wiry tentacular legs, which expose their scarlet linings and metal filaments. It is knitted yet solid, it raises a square jaw with a woollen beard and some teeth dripping with matted hair and broken hairpins, multicoloured fluffy foam and cotton spittle. Its eyes are bland blue rounds with soft chenille lashes. It is a Hoover and a dragon, inert and suffocating.

And the lady is flesh-coloured and twisted, her body is broken and concertinaed, she is draped flat on a large stone, her long limbs are pink nylon, her chains are twisted brassières and demented petticoats, pyjama cords and sinister strained tights. She has a cubist aspect, crossed with Diana of Ephesus again, her breasts are a string of detached and battered shoulder-pads, three above two, her pubic hair is shrunk angora bonnet. Her face is embroidered on petit-point canvas on a round embroidery-frame, it is half-done, a Botticelli Venus with a chalk outline, a few blonde tresses, cut-out eye-holes, stitched round with spiky black lashes. At first you think that the male figure is totally absent, and then you see him, them, minuscule in the crannies of the rock, a plastic knight on a horse, once silver, now mud-green, a toy soldier with a broken sword and a battered helmet, who have both obviously been through the wheel of the washing-machine, more than once.

There is someone in the window hanging a series of

letters, gold on rich chocolate, on a kind of hi-tech washing-line with tiny crimson pegs. It says,

SHEBA BROWN   WORK IN VARIOUS MATERIALS
1975-1990

Underneath the line of letters a photograph goes up. Debbie goes out into the street to look at it, a photograph of Mrs Brown under a kind of wild crown of woven scarves, with her old carved look and an added look of sly amusement, in the corners of mouth and eyes. Her skin has come out duskier than it 'really' is, her bones are sculpted, she resembles a cross between the Mona Lisa and a Benin bronze.

As far as Debbie knows, Mrs Brown is at this moment hoovering her stairs. She cannot think. She thinks several things at once. She thinks with pure delight of the unexpectedness and splendour of Sheba, for Mrs Brown. She thinks inconsequentially of a ball she once went to, a Chelsea Arts Ball, in the mulberry-coloured dress which is now the dragon-scales. She thinks, with a terrible flutter of unreadiness to think about this, that Mrs Brown will now for certain leave. She wonders why Mrs Brown said nothing—was it a desire to shock, or a

78

simpler desire to startle, or the courtesy of the old Mrs Brown, aware that Debbie could not do without her, thinking how to break the news, or was she—she certainly is in part—*simply* secretive and cautious? She thinks with terrible protectiveness of Robin in his attic, explaining his fetishes to Mrs Brown, and roaring as he will roar no more, about her forays into his workplace. She does not feel for a moment that Mrs Brown has 'stolen' Robin's exhibition, but she has a miserable fear that Robin may think that.

And she feels something else, looking at Sheba Brown's apparently inexhaustible and profligate energy of colourful invention. She feels a kind of subdued envy which carries with it an invigorating sting. She thinks of the feel of the wooden blocks she used to cut.

Tom Sprot comes up, full of excitement. He has discovered a chest of drawers full of tangled thread and smaller chests of drawers all full of tangled thread and smaller still chests of drawers. He has got the text of an interview done by an art critic for *A Woman's Place*, the text of which has just been delivered hot to the gallery by a messenger on a motorbike.

Debbie skims through it.

Sheba Brown lives in a council flat, surrounded by her own work, wall-hangings and cushions. She is in her forties, of part-Guyanese, part-Irish ancestry, and has had a hard life. Her work is full of feminist comments on the trivia of our daily life, on the boredom of the quotidian, but she has no sour reflections, no chip on her shoulder, she simply makes everything absurd and surprisingly beautiful with an excess of inventive wit. Some of her hangings resemble the work of Richard Dadd, with their intricate woven backgrounds, though they obviously owe something also to the luxurious innovations of Kaffe Fasset. But Sheba Brown, unlike Richard Dadd, is not mad or obsessed; she is richly sane and her conversation is good-humoured and funny.

She has brought up two sons, and gathered the materials for her work on a mixture of Social Security and her meagre earnings as a cleaner. She gets her materials from everywhere—skips, jumble sales, cast-offs, going through other people's rubbish, clearing up after school fêtes. She says she began on her 'soft sculpture' by accident really—she had an 'urge to construct' but had to make things that could be packed away into small spaces at night. Her two most prized possessions are a knitting-machine and a lockup room in the basement of her block of flats which she has by arrangement with the caretaker. 'Once I had the room, I could make box-like things as well as squashy ones,' she says, smiling with satisfaction.

Art Work

She says she owes a great deal to one family for whom she has worked, an 'artistic family' who taught her about colours (not that she needed 'teaching'—her instinct for new shocking effects and juxtapositions is staggering) and broadened her ideas of what a work of art might be . . .

Debbie goes home thoughtful. Mrs Brown has done her day's work and left. Robin is fretful. He does not want spaghetti for supper, he is sick of pasta, he thinks they must have had pasta every night for a fortnight. Debbie considers him, as he sits twisting his fettucine with a fork, and thinks that on the whole it is probably safe to tell him *nothing* about Mrs Brown and her Aladdin's Cave, since he never takes an interest in *A Woman's Place*, she can hide that from him, and she can probably keep other criticism from him too, he doesn't read much, it depresses him.

No sooner has she worked all this out than it is all ruined by Jamie, who rushes into the kitchen crying, come and see, come and see, Mrs Brown is on the telly. When neither of his parents moves he cries louder,

'She's got an exhibition of things like Muppets with that gallery-lady who came here, do come and look, Daddy, they're *bizarre*.'

So Robin goes and looks. Sheba Brown looks down her long nose at him out of the screen and says,

'Well, it all just comes to me in a kind of coloured rush, I just like putting things together, there's so much in the world, isn't there, and making things is a natural enough way of showing your excitement . . .'

The screen briefly displays the Hoover-dragon and the washing-bound lady.

'No, no, I don't do it out of *resentment*,' says Sheba Brown enthusiastically in voice-over, as the camera pursues the strangling twisted tights. 'No, I find it all *interesting*, I told you. Working as a cleaning-lady, OK, you learn a lot, it's honest, you can see things *anywhere at all* to make things up from, that's one thing I know. People are funny really, you can't be a cleaning-lady for long without learning that . . .'

Debbie looks at Robin. Robin looks at Sheba Brown. Sheba Brown vanishes and is replaced by a jolly avuncular Tar surrounded by simpering infants, brandishing a plateful of steaming rectangular Fishy Morsels. Robin says,

'That, round that woman-sort-of-thing's neck, that was that school tie I lost.'

'You didn't lose it. You threw it out.'

'No, I didn't. How would I have done that? I might go back to some school reunion, might I not, you never know, and it isn't likely I shall go and waste any money on *another* hideous purple tie, is it?'

'It was in the waste-paper basket. I said she could have it.'

'Mummy,' says Jamie, 'can we go and *see* Mrs Brown's squashy sculptures?'

'We will all go,' says Robin. 'Courtesy requires that we all go. And see what else she has filched.'

Mrs Brown comes in the next day accompanied by a grey-haired sylph in ballet tights and trainers.

'Mrs Brown, Mrs Brown,' says Jamie (it is the school holidays), 'Mrs Brown, we saw you on the telly. And your name is beautiful, and I think the Muppet sort of things and the little faces are stupiferous.'

Mrs Brown says,

'It looks as though I can't come for a bit, Mrs Dennison. I hadn't quite taken what a change in my life it was going to make, showing anyone my things. I just suddenly got it into my head that it was time they were seen by someone, you know how it is, and things got taken on from there, out of my control rather, though I'm not complaining. I kept meaning to say something, but it didn't seem to be the moment, and I was concerned for you, how you would take it, for you do need someone to rely on, as we both know. Now this here is Mrs Stimpson, who will do exactly what I did, I'll show her all the ropes, and how not to interfere with Mr Dennison, and I really do think you'll hardly notice, Mrs Dennison. It'll be just the same.'

Debbie stares silently at Mrs Brown. Mrs Brown drops her eyes and then looks up slightly flushed.

'You do see how it was?' she asks, steadily enough. Debbie thinks, the worst thing is, if we had been friends, she would have shown me her things. But we weren't. I only thought we were.

Sheba Brown says, 'We understood each other, Mrs Dennison. But no one's unique. Mrs Stimpson is quite reliable and resourceful. I wouldn't let you down by bringing anyone who wasn't. She'll be just like me.'

Debbie says, 'And does Mrs Stimpson make secret works of art?'

'Now *that*,' says Sheba Brown, 'you will have to find out for yourself.'

Mrs Stimpson's young-old face has a firm, knowing little smile on it. She says,

'We can but try, Mrs Dennison. Without prejudice.'

'I suppose so,' says Debbie. Before she can open her mouth again Mrs Brown and Mrs Stimpson have gone into the kitchen. Debbie hears the coffee-grinder. They will bring her a cup of coffee. It will all be more or less the same.

Or not quite the same. For one thing, Debbie goes back to making wood-engravings. *A Book of Bad Fairies* and *A Book of Good Fairies*, which have a certain success in the world of book illustration. Some of the more exotic fairies have the carved, haughty face of Sheba Brown, and the sweet, timeless face of Mrs Stimpson. And Robin? He roars at Mrs Stimpson, who humours him by appearing to be very flurried and rushing energetically to and fro at his behest. He also develops an interest in oriental mythology, and buys several books of tantric mandalas and prayer-wheels. One day Debbie goes up to his room and finds a new kind of painting on the easel, geometric, brightly coloured, highly organised, a kind of woven pattern of flames and limbs with a recurring motif of a dark, glaring face with red eyes and a protruding red tongue. 'Kali the Destroyer,' says Mrs Stimpson, knowledgeably at Debbie's elbow. 'It's a picture of Kali the Destroyer.' It is not right, thinks Debbie, that the black goddess should be a simplified travesty of Sheba Brown, that prolific weaver of bright webs. But at the same time she recognises a new kind of loosed, slightly savage energy in Robin's use of colour and movement. 'It's *got* something,' says Mrs Stimpson pleasantly. 'I do really think it's *got* something.' Debbie has to agree. It has indeed got something.

The Chinese Lobster

Nymphe et faune, 1931-2

The Chinese Lobster

The proprietors of the 'Orient Lotus' alternate frenetic embellishment with periods of lassitude and letting go. Dr Himmelblau knows this, because she has been coming here for quick lunches, usually solitary, for the last seven years or so. She chose it because it was convenient—it is near all her regular stopping-places, the National Gallery, the Royal Academy, the British Museum—and because it seemed unpretentious and quietly comfortable. She likes its padded seats, even though the mock leather is split in places. She can stack her heavy book-bags beside her and rest her bones.

The window on to the street has been framed in struggling cheese-plants as long as she can remember. They grow denser, dustier, and still livelier as the years go by. They press their cut-out leaves against the glass, the old ones holly-dark, the new ones yellow and shining. The glass distorts and folds them, but they press on. Sometimes there is a tank of coloured fish in the window, and sometimes not. At the moment, there is not. You can see bottles of soy sauce, and glass containers which dispense toothpicks, one by one, and chrome-plated boxes full of paper napkins, also frugally dispensed one by one.

Inside the door, for the last year or so, there has been a low square shrine, made of bright jade-green pottery, inside which sits a little brass god, or sage, in the lotus position, his comfortable belly on his comfortable knees. Little lamps, and sticks of incense, burn before him in bright scarlet glass pots, and from time to time he is decorated with scarlet and gold shiny paper trappings. Dr Himmelblau likes the colour-mixture, the bright blue-green and the saturated scarlet, so nearly the same weight. But she is a little afraid of the god, because she does not know who he is, and because he is obviously *really* worshipped, not just a decoration.

Today there is a new object, further inside the door, but still before the tables or the coathangers. It is a display-case, in black lacquered wood, standing about as high as Dr Himmelblau's waist—she is a woman of medium height—shining with newness and sparkling with polish. It is on four legs, and its lid and side-walls—about nine inches deep—are made of glass. It resembles cases in museums, in which you might see miniatures, or jewels, or small ceramic objects.

Dr Himmelblau looks idly in. The display is brightly lit, and arranged on a carpet of that fierce emerald-green artificial grass used by greengrocers and undertakers.

Round the edges on opened shells, is a border of raw scallops, the pearly flesh dulling, the repeating half-moons of the orange-pink roes playing against the fierce green.

In the middle, in the very middle, is a live lobster, flanked by two live crabs. All three, in parts of their bodies, are in feeble perpetual motion. The lobster, slowly in this unbreathable element, moves her long feelers and can be seen to move her little claws on the end of her legs, which cannot go forward or back. She is black, and holds out her heavy great pincers in front of her, shifting them slightly, too heavy to lift up. The great muscles of her tail crimp and control and collapse. One of the crabs, the smaller, is able to rock itself from side to side, which it does. The crabs' mouths can be seen moving from side to side, like scissors; all three survey the world with mobile eyes still lively on little stalks. From their mouths comes a silent hissing and bubbling, a breath, a cry. The colours of the crabs are matt, brick, cream, a grape-dark sheen on the claw-ends, a dingy, earthy encrustation on the hairy legs. The lobster was, is, and will not be, blue-black and glossy. For a moment, in her bones, Dr Himmelblau feels their painful life in the thin air. They stare, but do not, she supposes, see her. She turns on her heel and walks quickly into the body of the 'Orient Lotus'. It occurs to her that the scallops, too, are still in some sense, probably, alive.

The middle-aged Chinese man—she knows them all well, but knows none of their names—meets her with a smile, and takes her coat. Dr Himmelblau tells him she wants a table for two. He shows her to her usual table, and brings another bowl, china spoon, and chopsticks. The muzak starts up. Dr Himmelblau listens with comfort and pleasure. The first time she heard the muzak, she was dismayed, she put her hand to her breast in alarm at the burst of sound, she told herself that this was not after all the peaceful retreat she had supposed. Her noodles tasted less succulent against the tin noise, and then, the second or the third time, she began to notice the tunes, which were happy, banal, Western tunes, but jazzed up and sung in what she took to be Cantonese. 'Oh what a beautiful *morn*ing. Oh what a beautiful *day*. I've got a kind of a *feel*ing. Everything's *go*-ing my *way.*' Only in the incomprehensible nasal syllables, against a zithery plink and plunk, a kind of gong, a sort of bell. It was not a song she had ever liked. But she has come to find it the epitome of restfulness and cheerfulness. Twang, tinkle, plink, *plink*. A cross-cultural object, an occidental Orient, an oriental Western. She associates it now with the promise of delicate savours, of warmth, of satisfaction. The middle-aged Chinese man brings her a pot of green tea, in the pot she likes, with the little transparent rice-grain flowers in the blue and white porcelain, delicate and elegant.

She is early. She is nervous about the forthcoming conversation. She has never met her guest personally, though she has of course seen him, in the flesh and on the television screen; she has heard him lecture, on Bellini, on Titian, on Mantegna, on Picasso, on Matisse.

His style is orotund and idiosyncratic. Dr Himmelblau's younger colleagues find him rambling and embarrassing. Dr Himmelblau, personally, is not of this opinion. In her view, Perry Diss is always talking about something, not about nothing, and in her view, which she knows to be the possibly crabbed view of a solitary intellectual, nearing retirement, this is increasingly rare. Many of her colleagues, Gerda Himmelblau believes, do not *like* paintings. Perry Diss does. He loves them, like sound apples to bite into, like fair flesh, like sunlight. She is thinking in his style. It is a professional hazard, of her own generation. She has never had much style of her own, Gerda Himmelblau—only an acerbic accuracy, which is an *easy* style for a very clever woman who looks as though she ought to be dry. Not arid, she would not go so far, but dry. Used as a word of moderate approbation. She has long fine brown hair, caught into a serviceable knot in the nape of her neck. She wears suits in soft dark, not-quite-usual colours—damsons, soots, black tulips, dark mosses—with clean-cut cotton shirts, not masculine, but with no floppy bows or pretty ribbons—also in clear colours, palest lemon, deepest cream, periwinkle, faded flame. The suits are cut soft but the body inside them is, she knows, sharp and angular, as is her Roman nose and her judiciously tightened mouth.

She takes the document out of her handbag. It is not the original, but a photocopy, which does not reproduce all the idiosyncrasies of the original—a grease-stain, maybe butter, here, what looks like a bloodstain, watered-down at the edges, there, a kind of Rorschach stag-beetle made by folding an ink-blot, somewhere else. There are also minute drawings, in the margins and in the text itself. The whole is contained in a border of what appear to be high-arched wishbones, executed with a fine brush, in India ink. It is addressed in large majuscules

TO THE DEAN OF WOMEN STUDENTS
DR GERDA HIMMELBLAU

and continues in minute minuscules

from peggi nollett, woman and student.

It continues:

I wish to lay a formal complaint against the DISTINGUISHED VISITING PROFESSOR the Department has seen fit to appoint as the supervisor of my disertation on *The Female Body and Matisse.*

In my view, which I have already made plain to anyone who cared to listen, and specificly to Doug Marks, Tracey Avison, Annie Manson, and also to you, Dr Gerda Himmelblau, this person should never have been assigned to direct this work, as he is *completley out of sympathy* with its feminist project. He is a so-called EXPERT on the so-called MASTER of MODERNISM but what does he know about Woman or the internal conduct of the Female Body, which has always until now been MUTE and had no mouth to speak.

Here followed a series of tiny pencil drawings which, in the original, Dr Himmelblau could make out to be lips, lips ambiguously oral or vaginal, she put it to herself precisely, sometimes parted, sometimes screwed shut, sometimes spattered with what might be hairs.

His criticisms of what I have written so far have always been null and extremely agressive and destructive. He does not understand that my project is ahistorical and *need not involve* any description of the so-called development of Matisse's so-called style or approach, since what I wish to state is esentially *critical,* and presented from a *theoretical* viewpoint with insights provided from contemporary critical methods to which the cronology of Matisse's life or the order in which he comitted his 'paintings' is *totaly irelevant.*

However although I thought I should begin by stating my theoretical position yet again I wish at the present time to lay a spercific complaint of *sexual harasment* against the DVP. I can and will go into much more detail believe me Dr Himmelblau but I will set out the gist of it so you can see there is something here *you must take up.*

I am writing while still under the effect of the shock I have had so please excuse any incoherence.

It began with my usual dispirting CRIT with the DVP. He asked me why I had not writen more of the disertation than I had and I said I had not been very well and also preocupied with getting on with my art-work, as you know, in the Joint Honours Course, the creative work and the Art History get equal marks and I had reached a *very difficult stage* with the Work. But I had writen some notes on Matisse's *distortions* of the Female Body with respect especially to the spercificaly Female Organs, the Breasts the Cunt the Labia etc etc and also to his ways of acumulating Flesh on certain Parts of the Body which appeal to Men and tend to imobilise Women such as grotesquely swollen Thighs or protruding Stomachs. I mean to conect this in time to the whole tradition of the depiction of Female Slaves and Odalisques but I have not yet done the research I would need to write on this.

Also his Women tend to have no features on their faces, they are Blanks, like Dolls, I find this sinister.

Anyway I told the DVP what my line on this was going to

be even if I had not writen very much and he argued with me and went so far as to say I was hostile and full of hatred to Matisse. I said this was not a relevant criticism of my work and that Matisse was hostile and full of hatred towards women. He said Matisse was full of love and desire towards women (!!!!!) and I said *exactly* but he did not take the point and was realy quite cutting and undermining and dismisive and unhelpful even if no worse had hapened. He even said in his view I ought to fail my degree which is no way for a supervisor to behave as you will agree. I was so tense and upset by his atitude that I began to cry and he pated me on my shoulders and tried to be a bit nicer. So I explained how busy I was with my art-work and how my art-work, which is a series of mixed-media pieces called Erasures and Undistortions was a part of my criticism of Matisse. So he *graciously* said he would like to see my art-work as it might help him to give me a better grade if it contributed to my ideas on Matisse. He said art students often had dificulty expresing themselves verbally although he himself found language 'as sensuous as paint'. [It is not my place to say anything about his prose style but I could.] [This sentence is heavily but legibly crossed out.]

Anyway he came—*kindly*—to my studio to see my Work. I could see immediately he did not like it, indeed was repeled by it which I supose was not a surprise. It does not try to be agreable or seductive. He tried to put a good face on it and admired one or two *minor* pieces and went so far as to say there was a great power of feeling in the room. I tried to explain my project of *revising* or *reviewing* or *rearranging* Matisse. I have a three-dimensional piece in wire and plaster-of-paris and plasticine called *The Resistance of Madame Matisse* which shows her and her daughter being *tortured* as they *were* by the Gestapo in the War whilst *he* sits like a Buddha cutting up pretty paper with scissors. They wouldn't tell him they were being tortured in case it disturbed his *work*. I felt sick when I found out that. The torturers have got identical scissors.

Then the DVP got personal. He put his arm about me and hugged me and said *I had got too many clothes on. He said they were a depressing colour* and he thought I ought to take them all off and *let the air get to me.* He said he would like to see me in bright colours and that I was really a *very pretty girl* if I would let myself go. I said my clothes were a statement about myself, and he said they were a *sad statement* and then he grabed me and began kissing me and fondling me and stroking intimate parts of me—it was disgusting—I will not write it down, but I can describe it clearly, believe me Dr Himmelblau, if it becomes necesary, I can give chapter and verse of every detail, I am still shaking with shock. The more I strugled the more he insisted and pushed at me with his body until I said I would get the police the moment he let go of me, and then he came to his senses and said that in the *good old days* painters and models felt a bit of *human warmth and sensuality* towards each other in the studio, and I said, not in my studio, and he said, clearly not, and went off, saying it seemed to him *quite likely* that I should fail both parts of my Degree.

Gerda Himmelblau folds the photocopy again and puts it back into her handbag. She then reads the personal letter which came with it.

Dear Dr Himmelblau,

I am sending you a complaint about a horible experience I have had. Please take it seriously and please help me. I am so unhapy, I have so little confidence in myself, I spend days and days just lying in bed wondering what is the point of geting up. I try to live for my work but I am very easily discouraged and sometimes everything seems so black and pointless it is almost hystericaly funny to think of twisting up bits of wire or modeling plasticine. Why bother I say to myself and realy there isn't any answer. I realy think I might be better off dead and after such an experience as I have just had I do slip back towards that way of thinking of thinking of puting an end to it all. The doctor at the Health Centre said just try to snap out of it what does *he* know? He ought to listen to people he can't realy know what individual people might do if they did *snap* as he puts it out of it, anyway out of what does he mean, snap out of what? The dead are snaped *into* black plastic sacks I have seen it on television body bags they are called. I realy think a lot about being a body in a black bag that is what I am good for. Please help me Dr Himmelblau. I frighten myself and the contempt of others is the last straw snap snap snap snap.

Yours sort of hopefully,
Peggi Nollett.

Dr Himmelblau sees Peregrine Diss walk past the window with the cheese-plants. He is very tall and very erect—columnar, thinks Gerda Himmelblau—and has a great deal of well-brushed white hair remaining. He is wearing an olive-green cashmere coat with a black velvet collar. He carries a black lacquered walking-stick, with a silver knob, which he does not lean on, but swings. Once inside the door, observed by but not observing Dr Himmelblau, he studies the little god in his green shade, and then stands and looks gravely down on the lobster, the crabs, and the scallops. When he has taken them in he nods to them, in a kind of respectful acknowledgement, and proceeds into the body of the restaurant, where the younger Chinese woman takes his coat and stick and bears them away. He looks round and sees his host. They are the only people in the restaurant; it is early.

'Dr Himmelblau.'

'Professor Diss. Please sit down. I should have asked whether you like Chinese food—I just thought this place might be convenient for both of us—'

'Chinese food—well-cooked, of course—is one of the great triumphs of the human species. Such delicacy, such intricacy, such simplicity, and so *peaceful* in the ageing stomach.'

'I like the food here. It has certain subtleties one discovers as one goes on. I have noticed that the restaurant is frequented by large numbers of real Chinese people—families—which is always a good sign. And the fish and vegetables are always fresh, which is another.'

'I shall ask you to be my guide through the plethora of the menu. I do not think I can face Fried Crispy Bowels, however much, in principle, I believe in venturing into the unknown. Are you partial to steamed oysters with ginger and spring onions? So intense, so *light* a flavour—'

'I have never had them—'

'Please try. They bear no relation to cold oysters,

whatever you think of those. Which of the duck dishes do you think is the most succulent . . . ?'

They chat agreeably, composing a meal with elegant variations, a little hot flame of chilli here, a ghostly fragrant sweetness of lychee there, the slaty tang of black beans, the elemental earthy crispness of beansprouts. Gerda Himmelblau looks at her companion, imagining him willy-nilly engaging in the assault described by Peggi Nollett. His skin is tanned, and does not hang in pouches or folds, although it is engraved with crisscrossing lines of very fine wrinkles absolutely all over— brows, cheeks, neck, the armature of the mouth, the eye-corners, the nostrils, the lips themselves. His eyes are a bright cornflower blue, and must, Dr Himmelblau thinks, have been quite extraordinarily beautiful when he was a young man in the 1930s. They are still surprising, though veiled now with jelly and liquid, though bloodshot in the corners. He wears a bright cornflower-blue tie, in rough silk, to go with them, as they must have been, but also as they still are. He wears a corduroy suit, the colour of dark slate. He wears a large signet ring, lapis lazuli, and his hands, like his face, are mapped with wrinkles but still handsome. He looks both fastidious, and marked by ancient indulgence and dissipation, Gerda Himmelblau thinks, fancifully, knowing something of his history, the bare gossip, what everyone knows.

She produces the document during the first course, which is glistening viridian seaweed, and prawn and sesame toasts. She says,

'I have had this rather unpleasant letter which I must talk to you about. It seemed to me important to discuss it informally and in an unofficial context, so to speak. I don't know if it will come as surprise to you.'

Perry Diss reads quickly, and empties his glass of Tiger beer, which is quickly replaced with another by the middle-aged Chinese man.

'Poor little bitch,' says Perry Diss. 'What a horrible state of mind to be in. Whoever gave her the idea that she had any artistic talent ought to be shot.'

Don't say bitch, Gerda Himmelblau tells him in her head, wincing.

'Do you remember the occasion she complains of?' she asks carefully.

'Well, in a way I do, in a way. Her account isn't very recognisable. We did meet last week to discuss her complete lack of progress on her dissertation—she appears indeed to have *regressed* since she put in her proposal, which I am glad to say I was *not* responsible for accepting. She has forgotten several of the meagre facts she once knew, or appeared to know, about Matisse. I do not see how she can *possibly* be given a degree—she is ignorant and lazy and pigheadedly misdirected—and I felt it my duty to tell her so. In my experience, Dr Himmelblau, a lot of harm has been done by misguided kindness to lazy and ignorant students who have been cosseted and *nurtured* and never told they are not up to scratch.'

'That may well be the case. But she makes specific allegations—you went to her studio—'

'Oh yes. I went. I am not as brutal as I appear. I did try to give her the benefit of the doubt. That part of her account bears some resemblance to the truth—that is, to what I remember of those very disagreeable events. I did say something about the inarticulacy of painters and so on—you can't have worked in art schools as long as I have without knowing that some can use words and some can only use materials—it's interesting how you can't always predict *which*.

'Anyway, I went and looked at her so-called Work.

The phraseology is catching. "So-called". A pantechnicon contemporary term of abuse.'

'And?'

'The work is *horrible*, Dr Himmelblau. It disgusts. It desecrates. Her studio—in which the poor creature also eats and sleeps—is papered with posters of Matisse's work. *La Rêve. Le Nu rose. Le Nu bleu. Grande Robe bleue. La Musique. L'Artiste et son modèle. Zorba sur la terrasse*. And they have all been smeared and defaced. With what looks like *organic matter*—blood, Dr Himmelblau, beef stew or faeces—I incline towards the latter since I cannot imagine good daube finding its way into that miserable tenement. Some of the daubings are deliberate reworkings of bodies or faces—changes of outlines—some are like thrown tomatoes—probably *are* thrown tomatoes—and eggs, yes—and some are *great swastikas of shit*. It is appalling. It is pathetic.'

'It is no doubt meant to disgust and desecrate,' states Dr Himmelblau, neutrally.

'And what does that matter? *How can that excuse it?*' roars Perry Diss, startling the younger Chinese woman, who is lighting the wax lamps under the plate warmer, so that she jumps back.

'In recent times,' says Dr Himmelblau, 'art has traditionally had an element of protest.'

'*Traditional protest, hmph,*' shouts Perry Diss, his neck reddening. 'Nobody minds protest, I've protested in my time, we all have, you aren't the real thing if you don't have a go at being shocking, protest is *de rigeur, I know*. But what I object to here, is the shoddiness, the laziness. It *seems to me*—forgive me, Dr Himmelblau—but this—this *caca* offends something I do hold sacred, a word that would make that little bitch *snigger,* no doubt, but sacred, yes—it seems to me, that if she could have produced *worked copies* of those—those masterpieces—those shining—never mind—if she could have *done some work*—understood the blues, and the pinks, and the whites, and the oranges, yes, and the blacks too—and if she could still have brought herself to feel she must—must *savage* them—then I would have had to feel some respect.'

'You have to be careful about the word masterpieces,' murmurs Dr Himmelblau.

'Oh, I know all that stuff, I know it well. But you have got to listen to me. It can have taken at the maximum *half an hour*—and there's no evidence anywhere in the silly girl's work that she's ever spent more than that actually *looking at* a Matisse—she has no accurate memory of one when we talk, *none,* she amalgamates them all in her mind into one monstrous female corpse bursting with male aggression—she can't *see,* can't you see? And for half an hour's shit-spreading we must give her a degree?'

'Matisse,' says Gerda Himmelblau, 'would sometimes make a mark, and consider, and put the canvas away for weeks or months until he *knew* where to put the next mark.'

'I know.'

'Well—the—the shit-spreading may have required the same consideration. As to location of daubs.'

'Don't be silly. I *can see* paintings, you know. I did look to see if there was any wit in where all this detritus was applied. Any visual *wit,* you know, I know it's meant to be funny. There wasn't. It was just slapped on. It was horrible.'

'It was meant to disturb you. It disturbed you.'

'Look—Dr Himmelblau—whose side are you on? I've read your Mantegna monograph. *Mes compliments,* it is a *chef-d'oeuvre*. Have you *seen* this stuff? Have you for that matter *seen* Peggi Nollett?'

'I am not on anyone's *side*, Professor Diss. I am the Dean of Women Students, and I have received a formal complaint against you, about which I have to take formal action. And that could be, in the present climate, very disturbing for me, for the Department, for the University, and for yourself. I may be exceeding my strict duty in letting you know of this in this informal way. I am very anxious to know what you have to say in answer to her specific charge.

'And yes, I have seen Peggi Nollett. Frequently. And her work, on one occasion.'

'Well then. If you have seen her you will know that I can have made no such—no such *advances* as she describes. Her skin is like a *potato* and her body is like a *decaying potato*, in all that great bundle of smocks and vests and knitwear and penitential hangings. Have you seen her legs and arms, Dr Himmelblau? They are bandaged like mummies, they are all swollen with strapping and strings and then they are contained in nasty black greaves and gauntlets of plastic with buckles. You expect some awful yellow ooze to seep out between the layers, ready to be smeared on *La Joie de vivre*. And her hair, I do not think her hair can have been washed for some years. It is like a carefully preserved old frying-pan, grease undisturbed by water. You *cannot believe* I could have brought myself to touch her, Dr Himmel-blau?'

'It is difficult, certainly.'

'It is impossible. I may have told her that she would be better if she wore fewer layers—I may even, impru-dently—thinking, you understand, of potatoes—have said something about letting the air get to her. But I as-sure you that was as far as it went. I was trying against my instincts to converse with her as a human being. The rest is her horrible fantasy. I hope you will believe me, Dr Himmelblau. You yourself are about the only al-most-witness I can call in my defence.'

'I do believe you,' says Gerda Himmelblau, with a lit-tle sigh.

'Then let that be the end of the matter,' says Perry Diss. 'Let us enjoy these delicious morsels and talk about something more agreeable than Peggi Nollett. These prawns are as good as I have ever had.'

'It isn't so simple, unfortunately. If she does not with-draw her complaint you will both be required to put your cases to the Senate of the University. And the Uni-versity will be required—by a rule made in the days when university senates had authority and power and *money*—to retain QCs to represent both of you, should you so wish. And in the present climate I am very much afraid that whatever the truth of the matter, you will lose your job, and whether you do or don't lose it there will be disagreeable protests and demonstrations against you, your work, your continued presence in the Univer-sity. And the Vice-Chancellor will fear the effect of the publicity on the funding of the College—and the course, which is the only Joint Honours Course of its kind in London—may have to close. It is *not* seen by our profit-oriented masters as an essential part of our new—"Thrust", I think they call it. Our students do not con-tribute to the export drive—'

'I don't see why not. They can't *all* be Peggi Nolletts. I was about to say—have another spoonful of bamboo-shoots and beansprouts—I was about to say, very well, I'll resign on the spot and save you any further bother. But I don't think I can do that. Because I won't give in to lies and blackmail. And because that woman *isn't an artist*, and *doesn't work*, and *can't see*, and should not have a degree. And because of Matisse.'

'Thank you,' says Gerda Himmelblau, accepting the vegetables. And, 'Oh dear yes,' in response to the declaration of intent. They eat in silence for a moment or two. The Cantonese voice asserts that it is a beautiful *morn*ing. Dr Himmelblau says,

'Peggi Nollett is not well. She is neither physically nor mentally well. She suffers from anorexia. Those clothes are designed to obscure the fact that she has starved herself, apparently, almost to a skeleton.'

'Not a potato. A fork. A pin. A coathanger. I see.'

'And is in a very depressed state. There have been at least two suicide bids—to my knowledge.'

'Serious bids?'

'How do you define serious? Bids that would perhaps have been effective if they had not been well enough signalled—for rescue—'

'I see. You do know that this does not alter the fact that she has no talent and doesn't work, and can't see—'

'She *might*—if she were well—'

'Do you think so?'

'No. On the evidence I have, no.'

Perry Diss helps himself to a final small bowlful of rice. He says,

'When I was in China, I learned to end a meal with pure rice, quite plain, and to taste every grain. It is one of the most beautiful tastes in the world, freshly-boiled rice. I don't know if it would be if it was all you had every day, if you were starving. It would be differently delicious, differently haunting, don't you think? You can't describe this taste.'

Gerda Himmelblau helps herself, manoeuvres delicately with her chopsticks, contemplates pure rice, says, 'I see.'

'*Why Matisse?*' Perry Diss bursts out again, leaning forward. 'I can see she is ill, poor thing. You can *smell* it on her, that she is ill. That alone makes it unthinkable that anyone—that I—should *touch* her—'

'As Dean of Women Students,' says Gerda Himmelblau thoughtfully, 'one comes to learn a great deal about anorexia. It appears to stem from self-hatred and inordinate self-absorption. Especially with the body, and with that image of our own body we all carry around with us. One of my colleagues who is a psychiatrist collaborated

with one of your colleagues in Fine Art to produce a series of drawings—clinical drawings in a sense—which I
have found most instructive. They show an anorexic
person before a mirror, and what *we* see—staring ribs,
hanging skin—and what *she* sees—grotesque bulges,
huge buttocks, puffed cheeks. I have found these most
helpful.'

'Ah. *We* see coathangers and forks, and *she* sees potatoes and vegetable marrows. There is a painting in that.
You could make an interesting painting out of that.'

'Please—the experience is terrible to her.'

'Don't think I don't know. I am not being flippant, Dr
Himmelblau. I am, or was, a serious painter. It is not
flippant to see a painting in a predicament. Especially a
predicament which is essentially visual, as this is.'

'I'm sorry. I am trying to think *what to do*. The poor
child wishes to annihilate herself. *Not to be.*'

'So I understand. But *why Matisse?* If she is so obsessed with bodily horrors why does she not obtain em-
ployment as an emptier of bedpans or in a maternity
ward or a hospice? And if she must take on Art, why
does she not rework Giacometti into Maillol, or vice

versa, or take on that old goat, Picasso, who did things to women's bodies out of genuine *malice?* Why *Matisse?'*

'Precisely for that reason, as you must know. Because he paints silent bliss. *Luxe, calme et volupté.* How can Peggi Nollett bear luxe, calme et volupté?'

'When I was a young man,' says Perry Diss, 'going through my own Sturm und Drang, I was a bit bored by all that. I remember telling someone—my wife—it all was *easy and flat.* What a fool. And then, one day I saw it. I saw how hard it is to see, and how full of pure power, once seen. Not *consolation,* Dr Himmelblau, *life and power.'* He leans back, stares into space, and quotes,

> 'Mon enfant, ma soeur,
> Songe à la douceur
> D'aller là-bas vivre ensemble!
> Aimer à loisir
> Aimer et mourir
> Au pays qui te ressemble!—
> Là, tout n'est qu'ordre et beauté
> Luxe, calme et volupté.'

Dr Himmelblau, whose own life has contained only a modicum of luxe, calme et volupté, is half-moved, half-exasperated by the vatic enthusiasm with which Perry Diss intones these words. She says drily,

'There has always been a resistance to these qualities in Matisse, of course. Feminist critics and artists don't like him because of the way in which he expands male eroticism into whole placid panoramas of well-being. Marxists don't like him because he himself said he wanted to paint to please businessmen.'

'Businessmen and intellectuals,' says Perry Diss.

'Intellectuals don't make it any more acceptable to Marxists.'

'Look,' says Perry Diss. 'Your Miss Nollett wants to shock. She shocks with simple daubings. Matisse was cunning and complex and violent and controlled and *he knew he had to know exactly what he was doing.* He knew the most shocking thing he could tell people about the purpose of his art was that it was designed *to please and to be comfortable.* That sentence of his about the armchair is one of the most wickedly provocative things that has ever been said about painting. You can daub the whole of the Centre Pompidou with manure from top to bottom and you will *never* shock as many people as Matisse did by saying art was like an armchair. People remember that with horror who know nothing about the context—'

'Remind me,' says Gerda Himmelblau.

'"What I dream of, is an art of balance, of purity, of quietness, without any disturbing subjects, without worry, which may be, for everyone who works with the mind, for the businessman as much as for the literary artist, something soothing, something to calm the brain, something analogous to a good armchair which relaxes him from his bodily weariness . . ."'

'It would be perfectly honourable to argue that that was a very *limited* view—' says Gerda Himmelblau.

'Honourable but impercipient. Who is it that understands *pleasure*, Dr Himmelblau? Old men like me, who can only just remember their bones not hurting, who remember walking up a hill with a spring in their step like the red of the Red Studio. Blind men who have had their sight restored and get giddy with the colours of trees and plastic mugs and the *terrible blue* of the sky. Pleasure is *life*, Dr Himmelblau, and most of us don't have it, or not much, or mess it up, and when we see it in those blues, those roses, those oranges, that vermilion, we should fall down and worship—for it is *the thing itself*. Who knows a good armchair? A man who has bone-cancer, or a man who has been tortured, he can recognise a good armchair . . .'

'And poor Peggi Nollett,' says Dr Himmelblau. 'How can she see that, when she mostly wants to die?'

'Someone intent on bringing an action for rape, or whatever she calls it, can't be all that keen on death. She will want to savour her triumph over her doddering male victim.'

'She is *confused*, Professor Diss. She puts out messages of all kinds, cries for help, threats . . .'

'Disgusting art-works—'

'It is truly not beyond her capacities to—to take an overdose and leave a letter accusing you—or me—of horrors, of insensitivity, of persecution—'

'Vengefulness can be seen for what it is. Spite and malice can be seen for what they are.'

'You have a robust confidence in human nature. And you simplify. The despair is as real as the spite. They are part of each other.'

'They are failures of imagination.'

'Of course,' says Gerda Himmelblau. 'Of course they are. Anyone who could imagine the terror—the pain—of those who survive a suicide—against whom a suicide is *committed*—could not carry it through.'

Her voice has changed. She knows it has. Perry Diss does not speak but looks at her, frowning slightly. Gerda Himmelblau, driven by some pact she made long ago with accuracy, with truthfulness, says,

'Of course, when one is at that point, imagining others becomes unimaginable. Everything seems clear, and simple, and *single*; there is only one possible thing to be done—'

Perry Diss says,

'That is true. You look around you and everything is bleached, and clear, as you say. You are in a white box, a white room, with no doors or windows. You are looking through clear water with no movement—perhaps it is more like being inside ice, inside the white room. There is only one thing possible. It is all perfectly clear and simple and plain. As you say.'

They look at each other. The flood of red has subsided under Perry Diss's skin. He is thinking. He is quiet.

Any two people may be talking to each other, at any moment, in a civilised way about something trivial, or something, even, complex and delicate. And inside each of the two there runs a kind of dark river of unconnected thought, of secret fear, or violence, or bliss, hoped-for or lost, which keeps pace with the flow of talk and is neither seen nor heard. And at times, one or both of the two will catch sight or sound of this movement, in himself, or herself, or, more rarely, in the other. And it is like the quick slip of a waterfall into a pool, like a drop into darkness. The pace changes, the weight of the air, though the talk may run smoothly onwards without a ripple or quiver.

Gerda Himmelblau is back in the knot of quiet terror which has grown in her private self like a cancer over the last few years. She remembers, which she would rather not do, but cannot now control, her friend Kay, sitting in a heavy hospital armchair covered with mock-hide, wearing a long white hospital gown, fastened at the back, and a striped towelling dressing-gown. Kay is not looking at Gerda. Her mouth is set, her eyes are sleepy with drugs. On the white gown are scarlet spots of fresh blood, where needles have injected calm into Kay. Gerda says, 'Do you remember, we are going to the concert on Thursday?' and Kay says, in a voice full of stumbling ill-will, 'No, I don't, what concert?' Her eyes flicker, she looks at Gerda and away, there is something malign and furtive in her look. Gerda has loved only one person in her life, her schoolfriend, Kay. Gerda has not married, but Kay has—Gerda was bridesmaid—and Kay has brought up three children. Kay was peaceful and kindly and interested in plants, books, cakes, her husband, her children, Gerda. She was Gerda's anchor of sanity in a harsh world. As a young woman Gerda was usually described as 'nervous' and also as 'lucky to have Kay Leverett to keep her steady'. Then one day Kay's eldest daughter was found hanging in her father's shed. A note had been left, accusing her schoolfellows of bullying. This death was not immediately the death of Kay— these things are crueller and slower. But over the years, Kay's daughter's pain became Kay's, and killed Kay. She said to Gerda once, who did not hear, who remembered only later, 'I turned on the gas and lay in front of the fire all afternoon, but nothing happened.' She 'fell' from a window, watering a window-box. She was struck a glancing blow by a bus in the street. 'I just step out now and close my eyes,' she told Gerda, who said don't be silly, don't be unfair to busdrivers. Then there was the codeine overdose. Then the sleeping-pills, hoarded with careful secrecy. And a week after Gerda saw her in the hospital chair, the success, that is to say, the real death.

The old Chinese woman clears the meal, the plates veiled with syrupy black-bean sauce, the unwanted cold rice-grains, the uneaten mange-touts.

Gerda remembers Kay saying, earlier, when her pain seemed worse and more natural, and must have been so much less, must have been bearable in a way:

'I never understood how anyone *could*. And now it seems so clear, almost the only possible thing to do, do you know?'

'No, I don't,' Gerda had said, robust. 'You *can't do that* to other people. You have no right.' 'I suppose not,' Kay had said, 'but it doesn't feel like that.' 'I shan't listen to you,' Gerda had said. 'Suicide can't be handed on.'

But it can. She knows now. She is next in line. She has flirted with lumbering lorries, a neat dark figure launching herself blindly into the road. Once, she took a handful of pills, and waited to see if she would wake up, which she did, so on that day she continued, drowsily nauseated, to work as usual. She believes the impulse is wrong, to be resisted. But at the time it is white, and clear, and simple. The colour goes from the world, so that the only stain on it is her own watching mind. Which it would be easy to wipe away. And then there would be no more pain.

She looks at Perry Diss who is looking at her. His eyes are half-closed, his expression is canny and watchful. He has used her secret image, the white room, accurately; they have shared it. *He knows that she knows,* and what is more, she knows that he knows. How he knows, or when he discovered, does not matter. He has had a long life. His young wife was killed in an air-raid. He caused scandals, in his painting days, with his relations with models, with young respectable girls who had not previously been models. He was the co-respondent in a divorce case full of dirt and hatred and anguish. He was almost an important painter, but probably not quite. At the moment his work is out of fashion. He is hardly treated seriously. Like Gerda Himmelblau he carries inside himself some chamber of ice inside which sits his figure of pain, his version of kind Kay thick-spoken and malevolent in a hospital hospitality-chair.

The middle-aged Chinese man brings a plate of orange segments. They are bright, they are glistening with juice, they are packed with little teardrop sacs full of sweetness. When Perry Diss offers her the oranges she sees the old scars, well-made *efficient* scars, on his wrists. He says,

'Oranges are the real fruit of Paradise, I always think. Matisse was the first to understand orange, don't you agree? Orange in light, orange in shade, orange on blue, orange on green, orange in black—

'I went to see him once, you know, after the war, when he was living in that apartment in Nice. I was full of hope in those days, I loved him and was enraged by him and meant to outdo him, some time soon, when I had just learned this and that—which I never did. He was ill then, he had come through this terrible operation, the nuns who looked after him called him "le ressuscité".

'The rooms in that apartment were shrouded in darkness. The shutters were closed, the curtains were drawn. I was terribly shocked—I thought he *lived in the light*, you know, that was the idea I had of him. I blurted it out, the shock, I said, "Oh, how can you bear to shut out the light?" And he said, quite mildly, quite courteously, that there had been some question of him going blind. He thought he had better acquaint himself with the dark. And then he added, "and anyway, you know, black is the colour of light". Do you know the painting *La Porte noire*? It has a young woman in an armchair quite at ease in a peignoir striped in lemon and cadmium and . . . over a white dress with touches of cardinal red—her hair is yellow ochre and scarlet—and at the side is the window and the coloured light and behind—above—is the black door. Almost no one could paint the colour black as he could. Almost no one.'

Gerda Himmelblau bites into her orange and tastes its sweetness. She says,

'He wrote, "I believe in God when I work."'

'I think he also said, "I am God when I work." Perhaps he is—not my God, but where—where I find that. I was brought up in the hope that I would be a priest, you know. Only I could not bear a religion which had a tortured human body hanging from the hands over its altars. No, I would rather have *The Dance*.'

Gerda Himmelblau is gathering her things together. He continues,

'That is why I meant what I said, when I said that young woman's—muck-spreading—offended what I called sacred. What are we to do? I don't want her to—to punish us by self-slaughter—nor do I wish to be seen to condone the violence—the absence of *work*—'

Gerda Himmelblau sees, in her mind's eye, the face of Peggi Nollett, potato-pale, peering out of a white box with cunning, angry eyes in the slit between puffed eyelids. She sees golden oranges, rosy limbs, a voluptuously curved dark blue violin-case, in a black room. One or the other must be betrayed. Whatever she does, the bright forms will go on shining in the dark. She says,

'There is a simple solution. What she wants, what she has always wanted, what the Department has resisted, is a sympathetic supervisor—Tracey Avison, for instance—who shares her way of looking at things—whose beliefs—who cares about political ideologies of that kind—who will—'

'Who will give her a degree and let her go on in the way she is going on. It is a defeat.'

'Oh yes. It is a question of how much it matters. To you. To me. To the Department. To Peggi Nollett, too.'

'It matters very much and not at all,' says Perry Diss. 'She may see the light. Who knows?'

They leave the restaurant together. Perry Diss thanks Dr Himmelblau for his food and for her company. She is inwardly troubled. Something has happened to her white space, to her inner ice, which she does not quite understand. Perry Diss stops at the glass box containing the lobster, the crabs, the scallops—these last now decidedly dead, filmed with an iridescent haze of imminent putrescence. The lobster and the crabs are all still alive, all, more slowly, hissing their difficult air, bubbling, moving feet, feelers, glazing eyes. Inside Gerda Himmelblau's ribs and cranium she experiences, in a way, the pain of alien fish-flesh contracting inside an exo-skeleton. She looks at the lobster and the crabs, taking accurate distant note of the loss of gloss, the attenuation of colour.

'I find that *absolutely appalling*, you know,' says Perry Diss. 'And at the same time, exactly at the same time, I don't give a damn? D'you know?'

'I know,' says Gerda Himmelblau. She does know. Cruelly, imperfectly, voluptuously, clearly. The muzak begins again. '*Oh* what a *beau*tiful *morn*ing. *Oh* what a *beau*tiful *day*.' She reaches up, in a completely uncharacteristic gesture, and kisses Perry Diss's soft cheek.

'Thank you,' she says. 'For everything.'

'Look after yourself,' says Perry Diss.

'Oh,' says Gerda Himmelblau. 'I will. I will.'

THE GAME

A story of two sisters, Cassandra and Julia, once close, but now hostile strangers. Confronted by a man from their past, who they once both loved and suffered over, they struggle with each other toward a denouement that is both shocking and as inevitable as a classical tragedy.

Fiction/Literature/0-679-74256-5

SUGAR AND OTHER STORIES

This dazzling collection of short fiction explores the fragile ties between generations, the dizzying abyss of loss, and the elaborate memories we construct against it.

Fiction/Literature/0-679-74227-1

THE VIRGIN IN THE GARDEN

A wonderfully erudite entertainment about a brilliant and eccentric family, in which enlightenment and sexuality, Elizabethan drama and contemporary comedy, intersect richly and unpredictably.

Fiction/Literature/0-679-73829-0

Available at your local bookstore, or call toll-free to order:
1-800-793-2665 (credit cards only).